*Jeffrey McDonnell*

# A MOST REMARKABLE MURDERER

"The detective story is a form that John D. MacDonald rarely tries, but he handles it admirably in THE DROWNER. Private detective Paul Stanial investigates an "accidental" drowning and unearths fascinatingly complex tax frauds, some footnotes on the sexual mores of Florida and one of the most remarkable murderers in recent fiction—plus an understanding of himself that changes his future life. Good solid detection blends well with all the realistic observation of people and places that marks MacDonald's less formal suspense stories."

—Anthony Boucher
New York Sunday Times Book Review

Fawcett Gold Medal Books
by John D. MacDonald:

# THE DROWNER

## JOHN D. MACDONALD

FAWCETT GOLD MEDAL  •  NEW YORK

A Fawcett Gold Medal Book
Published by Ballantine Books

ISBN 0-449-12936-5

A shorter version of this novel appeared in *Cosmopolitan*
under the same title.

Printed in Canada

First Fawcett Gold Medal Edition: June 1963
Third Printing: July 1985

# One

ONE DAY after it was all over, after it was ended and done and there was no going back to change any part of it, Paul Stanial realized, checking the dates, that he and the Hanson woman had gone swimming on the same day, at the same hour, over a hundred miles apart, and had walked from the same noontime simmer of May in Florida, across sand into coolness. But on that day he had never heard of her, or even of the grove-country lake in which she had died that day.

Nevertheless, it had changed his life at a time it most desperately needed changing, and he found a strange significance in the fact that her swim in that silent lake had ended her life, and that his swim off that junk beach below Lauderdale had been part of the procedures that were sickening him, and had led him to demand the change which brought his life into tangent with hers, after hers was over.

His was a cool and watchful mind, full of measurements and dimensions, capable of fits of black rage over which he had achieved a precarious control, but not prone to make fanciful relationships between unrelated events. By the time he could see this fateful coincidence, he knew just how it had been for her. And though he never saw Lucille Hanson alive, by then he had talked to those who had known her, and he had seen where it had happened, and he knew the flavors of her mind and spirit from reading her letters. He saw it over and over, like an arbitrary eye suspended perhaps twenty feet above the shoreline of Dayker's Lake. He saw the old car nose down through the brush on the sand road in the bright noon-time heat and stop, facing the lake. He saw the woman get out, leaving the car door open, and take off her denim wrap-around skirt and toss it into the car. She wore a white swim suit and sandals. Her hair was fair, a golden white, and her body was tanned. Her rather narrow face, long throat, small breasts and long slender waist gave her a deceptive look of fragility. But there was a sturdy breadth to her round strong hips, and her thighs and calves were round-ed and heavy. He saw her mash a mosquito against the top of a solid thigh, and reach into the car, get her gear, slam the car door and walk quickly to the edge of the small sandy beach. He saw her spread her towel, put the other articles down, step out of her sandals, and then walk to the water, tucking her pale hair into the blue swim cap, her expression that of a woman alone, slightly solemn, preoccupied, thinking of the two men who loved her, perhaps, and the one she loved.

And then the objective eye turned and he saw her swim out, the strong legs pumping, the arms reaching smoothly, the head turning at the right beat to take the deep easy breath. From that vantage point he watched just how it was done to her, saw how she was given no chance at all. He watched below then, down in the amber murk of twenty feet, watched her come down slowly and alone when it was over for her, turning, unmarked except for that emptiness of death upon her face, sinking to the weeds and mud of the bottom, re-bounding slightly, turning in a random current, and then settling, sprawled on her side, eyes open, an edge of white teeth showing, a last reflex moving the left hand, some gassy bubbles and then weedy silence in the brown-gold depths.

But his own swim that same day, that same hour, on a trashy dazzle of beach at Hallandale, adjacent to glossy mo-tels, had been entirely different in flavor. The agency had used him on this one because, he realized with a certain sourness, he looked enough like the other beach bums to be next to invisible in the throng. His natural skin tone was dark enough to take and hold a deep tan. His hair was black and his deep-set eyes a clear, bright blue. He was tall and long-legged, with flat hips, a lithe, narrow waist, but a deep chest, short broad neck, and wide, heavily muscled shoul-ders. From a distance his trimness made him look years younger than he was.

The assignment was a soft, beefy, youngish man from Bloomfield Hills, Michigan, named Geoffrey Rogers. He had married a monied woman who was anxious to divorce him, but Rogers was holding out for a private settlement before agreeing. They'd been given the word he was taking a little break in the Miami area with a blonde hostess from a Detroit night spot. The office had traced him through the phone number he had given the airlines for his return reservation,

and had found him holed up in cabana unit G of the Beach-
scape Motel, registered as Mr. and Mrs. R. Jeffries of Lan-
sing.

Paul Stanial had been detailed to pick up all the client
would need to pry herself loose from Rogers with minimum
expense. So he checked into the cheapest single at the Beach-
scape so as to have the run of the place and the beach. He
wired a battery-driven, 35-millimeter camera into a small
green plastic tackle box, loaded with a 36-exposure roll of
Kodachrome, and cut a hole under the side latch for the
wide-angle lens. He cut another hole on top next to the
carrying handle, big enough so he could stick his index
finger through it and punch the shutter button. Properly set
for bright sunlight, he was in focus from four feet to infinity,
and the wide-angle simplified the aiming problem. They
were so sexually engrossed in each other, he was in no
danger of being detected as he took his shots of them, some
from as close as five feet. She was a vapid-faced woman with
a rich body just beginning to go to seed. They sprawled and
necked on their beach towels in a meaty abandon, while he
sunned nearby and caught some of the more incriminating
pawings. He took them leaving and entering their cabana,
and he got one on the terrace of the cabana with Rogers
supine on a white sun chaise, the woman straddling his
thighs, facing him, leaning toward him, his hand under her
bikini top and her hand rammed up the leg of his swim
trunks. Moments later they got up and went into the cabana and drew the draperies across the picture window.
Stanial put the camera in his room and went for a swim. He
swam out and floated on the swells and wondered how many
waves it would take to wash away the stink of that pair, and
suddenly he knew he couldn't take much more of this kind
of assignment. Something had to change before he found he
had stopped giving a damn what he had to do, so long as
he was paid.

He took the film to a special order lab, asked for one
color slide of each exposure, and waited fifty minutes in an
air-conditioned bar down the street while they ran it through
the electronic processing equipment. He signed the charge
slip, went out and sat on a bench and held each slide up to
the light. They were no example of the art of photography,
but they clearly established the identities and the specific
relationship between the pair.

He went back to the office and turned the slides and

the photostat of the registration over to Kippler and sat while Kippler looked carefully at each picture.

"This broad is really stacked," Kippler murmured. "And eager. Say, this one nails it good, her opening the door and the number showing up good on the door, and him with the towels and stuff. By the way, Charlie got a Thermofax of the car rental sheet. Rogers used his own name on that so he could use his credit card." He pursed his lips and studied one picture. "There's too much in focus, so it wasn't tele-photo. What'd you do, fella? Join the group?"

"Is that the next step?"

Kippler looked at him thoughtfully. "What's chewing you?"

"I've had too much of this kind of thing, one after the other. I'm fed up to here with it. Is this the only kind of business you get down here?"

"It's a big part of it."

"For God's sake, get me some cop work so I can live with myself for a little while. I've got cop training. This kind of assignment sickens me."

"So maybe you're a little stale, Paul. Try B and B. Broad and bottle."

"Let me ask you one question, Mr. Kippler. Am I worth hanging onto?"

"You're working out pretty good here."

"Then please assign me to something more like police work, and soon, or I'm going to have to get out. I don't care if it's something that checks out to be nothing at all, just so long as I get a change from the bedroom circuit."

"You're working in the world's biggest bedroom."

"I can take it, if I get a change once in a while."

Kippler sighed. "I shouldn't do this. But the very next thing that comes along, you get it. The thing I have for you now, I don't even want to show you the file until you're in a better mood. So come in in the morning, and best of all, come in with a slight hangover, Paul."

And so, that evening, thinking Kippler's advice might do some good, he dated a girl he knew slightly. They cruised the beach and had a little too much to drink and he kept telling himself he was having a good time, that he was relaxing. He went back with her to her small apartment on the mainland, and as soon as they were inside the small living room, before she had turned a light on, she turned hard into his arms and broke her mouth upward against his in a breathless hunger, dug her nails into his back and canted her body into him in total, unmistakable presentation of herself. For a moment it was fine, until suddenly in the darkness she was the very same woman Rogers had been enjoying, the same woman he had seen over and over again, in different shapes and sizes.

He pushed her away and went clumping down the stairs, hearing the anger and the disappointment in her voice as she called his name. He drove without thought of destination, left the city and drove north for an hour and found a beach road, a tract for sale, parked and walked through the sea oats and rough grasses to an empty starlit beach, and a sound of surf.

He sat on the dry sand and tasted the seawind. The fuzziness of the drinks had faded away, but he felt caught in the torment of an agony he could not define, akin to the yearnings of the adolescence a decade and a half behind him. He knew out of a cumulative knowledge that Paul Stanial could not survive much longer as this particular human being unless he found his own meaning again. He wanted prideful work, to use all his skills, all his energies and abilities. And he wanted a woman to go with the work. A woman who knew what he was and what he needed, so that he in turn could give himself to her. So that there could be a communication beyond words and rituals. Not a child-woman who knew none of the tastes and terrors of the world. Nor one hardened by too many emotional abrasions. Just a woman of taste and sensitivity, of such restraint she would not give of herself until she knew the extent of the gift would be known, and then would give deeply and gladly and forever, knowing she would be cherished. Is this, he wondered, too puerile, too romantic an image? I don't want a breath-taking beauty. I want her to value herself, and me. And I want to value her and my work. I want some damned purpose, some dedication.

Once he had thought he had the job and the woman, but they had both soured. Now, he realized, with some bitterness, that he was living the daydream of ten million men— to be single, mature, husky, well-paid and have a job in the Miami area with freedom of movement and the chance to develop all the contacts any man could use.

He looked south where the sky reflected the pink-white glow of the Lauderdale, Hallandale, Miami complex. Sure, fellas. Break all ties and come on down. The biggest hedonistic complex in the known world. One big noisy sunny cauldron of busy butts and ripe red mouths, rare steaks and guitars, skinny-dipping and party games, twisters and gin, kicks and tits, laughter and brass horns, oiled brown backs and tall teased hair. Wade in, guys. Welcome to the most concentrated, gut-wrenching loneliness ever devised by man.

After a long time he stood up and stretched until the hard muscles of his shoulders popped and creaked, yawned until his jaw ached. The last resentment, he thought. One final day of yearning for what might have been. Then he spat into the sand and headed back to the car.

Later, after he knew all that was worth knowing about the life and death of Lucille Hanson, he was to remember that day and that evening. It was all beginning then, of course. Perhaps a good starting place was in the afternoon, when that old musician walked down to the boathouse to tell Kelsey Hanson his wife was dead. . . .

Kelsey Hanson, all hungers appeased and brute-softened muscles relaxed, lay snorting in his sleep on a white sun cot on the second floor cypress sun deck of an elaborate boathouse overlooking Lake Larra. He wore brief shiny blue trunks. The hero mouth hung open.

Between her little drowsings there on the big beach towel spread on the cypress planking of the floor, the naked girl looked at him without enthusiasm. She was nineteen, and a student at the local college. Her name was Shirley Feldman. She wished Kelsey could sleep a little more attractively. She yawned and steeped herself in the languor of the afternoon sun, hidden from the world by the wooden wall around the sun deck. Sweaty-sweet, limber-small of waist, usefully round of hip, she was a breasty, brown, sturdy little girl with a face narrow and sensitive and small under the hard mushroom mop of black hair. The sun was a hearty and indifferent weight against her body, yet with a hot sly touch on the places it seldom reached. Her pumpkin-colored play suit, her scuffed sandals and sensible underwear lay spilled a yard away, efficiently shed in a four-breath hiatus between the wine and the loving.

If only he didn't sleep like . . . like a slob. It confused the images, she thought. It made her feel used. There was a choice of patterns. The older man—he was at least thirty—seeks a new clarity of vision through the eyes of an intellectual woman, able to detect the fraudulence of his emotional attitudes and postures and point them out to him in reasoned statement. Mid-century man, without direction, re-examining his male purposes. That made it the project pattern, the one she had discussed at such length with Debbie. But when Debbie had given up and—in a sense—passed him along, Debbie had claimed the whole thing was just a sales posture, saying that Hanson had signed up for a few courses and had hung around the college merely to score with the gullible ones that would believe the lost lamb attitude. But there had to be more to him than that. Debbie had failed because she didn't have the patience to get past his defenses. Debbie said, with an ugly mouth, he could cry on cue by thinking of sliced onions.

If such was actually his hunger, then that could be another project in itself, to show him that it was not that important, that he was victimized by a socio-sexual trauma based on some puritanical and primitive consciousness of sin. Liberated by her freedom from sex superstitions, and by a disc of latex, she had certainly showed him, time and again, that it was merely a healthy and companionable reflex, with the cues given in a cheery voice so that a proper and skilful and earnest climax could be achieved; not something to get all knotted up about, sickly and guilt-ridden, not something shameful. That damned priss wife of his had probably contributed more than her share to his emotional shambles. So it was a pleasant, unimportant and gratifying task to prove to him that total honesty was really the ultimate innocence.

But she wondered why it would all make more sense were he not such a sloppy sleeper.

Then you could take it hedonistically. The muscles, money and Mercedes, the steaks and wine and speedboat certainly made the tropical life one hell of a lot more instructive for a scholarship student with an impressive IQ far from her New Jersey beginnings. Stay trapped on campus and you might as well have gone to CCNY.

She wished he could look defenseless and childlike while sleeping. Then it would all be better. Asleep he looked like a cigar smoker at a convention hotel. It gave her a feeling she could not define. An unrest.

In the hot silence of the afternoon she suddenly heard the slow, ascending clump of footsteps on the outside staircase that led from the ground level up to the sun deck and living quarters. She sat up abruptly, rigid and breathless in a panic which astonished her. Then, from the labored cadence of the footsteps, she knew it was the old composer to whom the elder Hansons had loaned the big house before going on their cruise around the world. She stood up slowly and lifted the big gaudy towel and wrapped it around her body, overlapping it above her breasts and tucking it in, in sarong fashion. Giving an old creature like Habad Korody free food and lodging was a pathetic and typical gesture—a yen for culture.

She had looked him up. He had enjoyed a small vogue a generation ago. He was a dusty footnote in musical history. The fiction was, of course, that he would live in the big house and compose while they were gone. If he dropped dead, no one would install a plaque on the spot.

He reached the top of the stairs and paused a moment for breath, staring at her. He wore a big planter's hat, sandals and oversized khaki shorts. His ancient body was skeletal, the parchment-brown hide dried against sinew and bone. There was a tuft of pure white hair in the center of his narrow hollow chest. The shrewd old monkey-eyes gleamed out at her from under the wide brim of the straw hat.

"What do *you* want?" she asked in a low scornful voice.

"I come with a message for the king, O maiden fair," he said and trudged over to the sun cot and stabbed Hanson cruelly in the softness of his waist with the iron spike of the musician's finger.

Kelsey erupted out of his sleep, bubbling and snarling and dazed. He sat up and stared at the old man. "What the hell?" he asked vacantly.

"Your phone here doesn't work and so they bothered me at the big house, please would I walk down and tell you. Go to the hospital. Something about your wife. Go talk to somebody named Walmo."

"Lucille? Something happened to Lucille?"

"I've told you all I was told."

After a motionless moment, Kelsey Hanson gathered himself and raced into the living quarters, leaving the sliding glass door open. The old man stared at Shirley. "Such a college," he said. "Such an education."

"It isn't anything to you. Who ever heard of you?"

The old man gave her a simian grin. "Defiance! Anger! Who's attacking?"

Hanson came hurrying back out in slacks and a sports shirt. He looked blankly at them and started toward the stairs, patting his pockets.

"What about me!" the girl yelled angrily. "What about me?"

Hanson paused and turned back and thrust a ten-dollar bill at her. It fluttered out of her grasp. "Call a cab," he said and ran down the stairs. His car roared, spewed gravel, whined away up the curving drive.

She picked up the money and picked up her clothes. "You delivered your message, old man."

He looked at her. "And another for you. If it matters. The human voice is an instrument without subtlety. It wasn't said on the phone, but it was obvious. The wife is dead."

The heat of the sun had a different quality. It made her flesh crawl. "You know everything," she said.

He shrugged. "I know about little ones like you. Smart little ones. Nothing changes. A little time of defiance and guilt, playing with an empty man like that one. Then you get pulled back to what you thought you were getting away from, girl. The things you think you despise. Home, husband, babies. Fruitful."

"You don't know anything about me!"

"I knew you forty years ago, and you haven't changed. His wife is dead. Put on your clothes. Comb your hair. Come to the big house and call a taxi."

He turned and went to the stairs and stomped slowly down, hanging onto the railing.

# Two

SAM KIMBER slouched in the oak chair in Sheriff Walmo's bare office and said in a tired voice, "Harv, you giving me the idea you're getting too damn diligent about a drowning. It's hard enough on me as it is, and you know it."

Harv Walmo shook his big head sadly. He had two habitual expressions, sadness and heartbreak. "I know it and can't help it, Sam. We just got to trace out where Miz Hanson was and why. You see any stenographer here taking notes? This is just you and me. Now what was your exact relationship to the decedent?"

"Dear Jesus," Sam Kimber said softly. He was a long gnarled knuckly powerful pale-eyed man with a lazy effortless look of importance. "You can answer it yourself. My exact relationship was she was my woman, as everybody guessed and nobody could prove."

Walmo moved and aligned papers on his desk. "When did this intimate relationship with the decedent begin?"

Sam Kimber jerked himself erect and stared at Harv with astonishment and anger. "Now just exactly what the . . ." He stopped suddenly, aware of the little flags and signals and alarms in the back of his mind. In a moment the equation was clear. Because they had always known each other, since earliest memory, he had made Harv an exception to his working rule that all friendships were conditional and limited. From the years of hunting, fishing, gambling, drinking and wenching with Harv Walmo, and due to the small pressures he had exerted which had gotten Harv elected sheriff some years back, he had thought the friendship was something true and lasting for them both. He looked into Harv's sad eyes and saw a little shift and glint back in there, a satisfaction, and knew it was his first clue in all these years to a hidden store of jealousy and resentment. It saddened Sam Kimber. So this too was false. And here and now, for the first time in all these years, Harv Walmo had his chance to lean a certain amount of unpleasant weight on his benefactor, and he was enjoying it. Because, after all, they had started even, and Harv would have to believe all of it was luck, not that Sam was the better man.

Sam slouched again, crossed his ankles, grinned at Harv with a wicked amiability and said, "Now any other man owning so much grove land and developments and little pieces of this and that around these here three counties, a sheriff starting to get feisty, he'd stand on his rights and yell for a lawyer. But you and me, we're friends all our life, Harv. Isn't that so?"

"I'm just . . ."

"Doing your sworn duty to the people voted you into office, and I respect you for it. I'm right proud to have for a friend a man who'll put his duty way to hell and gone ahead of his chance of getting re-elected."

Walmo was motionless for a moment. "You never said a thing like that to me before, Sam."

"You never give me cause. It's a hot month and a hot day, and time we stopped wearing each other out and got back to making sense. You want me to talk about Lucille, I'll talk about Lucille. And things will be just the way they were."

Which, Sam thought, we both know is a damn lie, but one we'll have to live by from here on.

"I'd like for you to tell me, Sam," Walmo said.

"It goes against me to talk about a woman. Any little ol' swamp kitten is good for a story, like them two down to Arcadia that time, remember? But Lucille, she's been something else. I knew her before she and Hanson split up, but didn't think much about her one way or another, just she was a real pretty young woman he found up there in Boston and married and brang down here, and the two of them partying around with the rest of the hard-drinking young ones. It was all over town how they come to split up, so you must have heard it told one way or another, and you might as well know the truth of it as she told it to me. Eleven months ago it was, April last year, time they went out of Stuart over to Bimini with the Keavers on that big Huckins he had then. Three years married, and him drinking hard and playing around and her waiting and hoping for him to grow up and turn into a man. Jase and Bonny Yates were with them at first and then had to fly back. I think it was the next day they took the boat around and were anchored off some beach, and she and Stu Keaver went to the beach in the dinghy leaving Kelse and Lorna Keaver aboard. She took it in her head to swim back and she went up the boarding ladder, quiet without meaning to, and caught Kelse and Lorna having at it. She made a big stink, and Lorna and Kelse didn't seem as upset as she thought they ought to be. And when Stu came back aboard and got the picture, he didn't act too agitated either. Everybody had a couple drinks and then a kind of kidding started she couldn't understand at first and all of a sudden she realized they were trying to talk her into putting out for Stu Keaver. Like she told me she was all of a sudden stone cold sick sober, looking at their animal eyes and all the smirking and dirty talk going on, and she knew she was a stranger in a strange place and it was all over for her."

"Dear Lord," Harv Walmo said.

"Soon as they got back to the Bimini dock, she got off with her gear and flew on Mackey back to Lauderdale and back to here, and by the time he could catch up she'd moved out of the big house, into the Orangeland Motel, getting set to head back north. He came around whining and begging and promising, but she said it didn't move her one inch. Except finally she agreed, trying to be fair, she'd settle for a legal separation for one year, and she'd stay in the county, and he'd support her, and if nothing had changed by the end of the year, then she'd go ahead with a Florida divorce, and he agreed because it was the best he could do with her, the mood she was in. She was going to file next month."

"How was that going to set with his folks?" Harv asked.

"Good question, and I guess you could answer it yourself. The old lady adores him, and she's been thinking of all this as just a little marriage spat, but old John Hanson has had the idea a long time his only son isn't worth the rope it would take to hang him. Old John liked Lucille, and he figured it was Kelsey's last chance to turn into anything at all. If the divorce had gone through, old John was going to finally heave Kelse out of the nest for good, no matter how much fuss the old lady put up. But now I don't know. When they left to go around the world last February, old John put Kelse in charge of the groves, but if he's been out there twice I'd be surprised."

"Then you got friendly with Lucille after she moved out?"

"Over a month afterward, Harv. She'd moved into that apartment in the old Carey place on Lemon Street, and she'd just started working mornings, reception work for Doc Nile. Kelse wasn't being too regular about the support, but she had some cash money she could take out of a trust thing up north, seventy-one hundred and some dollars, and she had the idea if she could put it to work down here it would be maybe a little more income. She'd heard all the rumors about everything I touch turning to money, and we'd met socially a couple times, so she came to the office for advice. I told her I wasn't any investment adviser. Truth of the matter, I figured her for just another one of that crowd, the Yates and the Keavers and the Bryes and all. Maybe I was a little rough, and it was like a last straw for her, and she put her face in her hands and started snuffling. Pretty young woman. That light hair and all. So I softened up and rode her around some looking at this and that, and she told me a little at a time how her dreams had gone to hell in a hand basket. So I took her in on that warehouse thing, a seven thousand piece of it that started bringing her ninety a month right off. We felt good being with each other, and I could talk easier to her than almost anybody. Because we were together so much, the talk started, but nothing went on between us, me forty-seven with growed children and Kitty dead since fifty-three, and her just twenty-seven. You got an anxious look in your eye, Harv, and you look a little sweaty, but you better settle back down because I'm giving you no details. I was in Jacksonville for the hearings, staying over a weekend for law talk, alone in a hotel room, depressed on account of how they fixing to chew me up up there, and so I just reached out and took the phone and called her, woke her out of bed at eleven at night on a Friday and told her I was so low I could walk under a gator without taking off my hat, and told her where I was and to get to me the fastest way she knew how. There was a long long silence and then a little click of her hanging up. Late Saturday I came dragging back from all that tax talk and went in and there she was setting in my room, pale as chalk. Tried to smile and tried to say something, but the tears just started running down her face. I don't know about love, Harv. It's a word gets kicked around. We never waved it in folks' faces. We made each other feel good, and she was more woman than you'd figure her for. I don't know if I would have married her because it never did come up. But I know I'm going to miss her long as I live."

After a long silence Harv moistened his lips and said, "Yesterday?"

"We'd spent the night out to that shack of mine beyond Beetle Creek and had two cars there on account of me having to go early to Lakeland on business, and her coming in to work. I wanted her to quit working but she said if she did she'd feel trampy. Never would take a dime from me, nor any present except little stuff, and gave me much as I gave her. She left first and I wrenched off the breakfast stuff and went on off to Lakeland. When I got back to town, got out of the car, first man I see is Charlie Best. About three o'clock, and he said she was dead. I couldn't make my legs work, see clear or think straight. And got as drunk last night as I've ever been."

"Did she say what she was going to do after she left Doc's office at noon?"

"We were supposed to go to a movie at the drive-in yesterday night, and I was to pick her up at the apartment along about six to eat first. I don't remember her saying anything about what she was going to do in the afternoon."

"Did you ever go swimming there with her?"

"I'm not much for swimming, as you know, Harv. We took picnics there a few times, and I'd watch her swim. I'd joke her a little about that place, saying as how it was land I'd

held onto long enough and I was going to get it platted up
and sold off. Too many people using it, littering it up. She'd
never quite know if I was serious. She'd swim and we'd eat
the picnic and she'd take her a little nap in the sun while
I'd watch over her, thinking on how lucky a man could get
sometimes."

"She was a good swimmer they say."

"She slid easy through the water and was never puffing
when she come wading out."

"This is just a routine investigation, Sam."

"Like you keep saying, Harv." Sam Kimber rose slowly to
his full six and a half feet. "One little favor I want to ask
you, Harv. Lucille and me, we got to trust each other pretty
good. With this tax persecution and all, she was doing a
little private book work for me, and it's some records I
need. I want to get into that apartment and get them."

"Where are they? I'll see you get them, Sam."

"I don't rightly know. I told her not to leave them laying
around."

"What do they look like?"

"Suppose you just clear it so as I can go get my records,
Harv."

Sam waited, hoping his tone had been convincingly casual.
Until today he wouldn't have been as wary of Harvey Walmo.
But Harv had turned into an unknown quantity. He wondered
if the tax suit had anything to do with it. He could guess the
rumors Harv had probably heard. Sam Kimber is in bad trouble. They're trying to nail him for fraud, and if they do,
they'll strip him clean and maybe even send him up. But if
that was the way Harv was thinking, he was in for an unpleasant surprise after all the dust settled. Sure, the Jacksonville boys were threatening fraud, but they didn't have much
chance of making it stick in court. It was just a big difference
of opinion on how some things should have been handled.
They'd built their case quietly the way they always do, and
then sprung the big audit and asked for eight hundred and
twenty-two thousand dollars, back taxes, penalties and
interest. Coming up with that would really strip him down.
But what you did was swing your own tax boys and legal
boys onto the firing line and start dickering. Their latest demand was about three hundred and forty thousand, and the
counter offer was a hundred and seventy thousand, with
three months to raise it in cash money. Gus Gable guessed
the compromise settlement would be in the neighborhood

of two hundred and twenty-five thousand. After all, as Gus had explained, they had the complete and detailed personal balance sheet, and to demand much more than that would force Sam to divest himself of so many income-producing properties, they'd be killing off the goose they expected to keep producing those golden eggs in future years. It would be a squeeze to raise that much, of course, but it could be done without upsetting any apple carts.

But there was that one little item he'd sneaked out from under them, the one that if it appeared on the personal balance sheet would go right into the kitty, right into Uncle's waiting hands. And that was the hundred and six thousand cash money. When they'd jumped him, they'd gotten court orders sealing the boxes they knew about, but they'd missed the two prime ones, mostly because Sam had been so careful about setting them up. So he'd taken the quick trips to Waycross and Pensacola, and packed the cash into the little blue airlines bag and then wondered exactly what the hell to do with it. And after considering and discarding a dozen frail plans, he'd merely turned it over to Lucille and told her to hide it in the apartment, and to quiet her curiosity he told her it was cash money, but not how much. He told her it was land promotion syndicate money entrusted to him on a deal so secret there weren't any papers of verification around, and he couldn't take the risk of it being grabbed by the tax people and used as evidence of fraud against him. He said he could prove it wasn't his, but in so doing he'd have to say so much he'd spoil the deal they were working on.

This satisfied her and she said she'd put it in a safe place and forget it. It was funny, he thought as he watched Harv make up his mind, that having Lucille gone made the money a lot less important. There were a lot less things to do with it, somehow. But it was a good big piece of cash, a useful tool for future ventures.

Harv sighed and wrote a note to Mrs. Carey asking her to let Sam into the apartment to get some personal items. He handed the note to Sam, saying, "I told her to keep it locked up until the law tells me who the stuff in there belongs to. She'll have folks coming down. I guess they'll work it out with Hanson."

After he had firmly, politely, smilingly closed the door in

Mrs. Carey's face and he was alone in the small apartment, Sam Kimber suddenly felt sick and weak. He sat on the couch, and he could imagine that at any moment he would hear the clink of dishes in the small kitchen and then that tuneless little happy humming sound of hers, the tock of her heels on linoleum. The apartment held no sensual memories. She had firmly labeled it out of bounds. But her presence was almost tangible. And it was worse when he began his search with the bedroom closet. There was a scent of her there, and her clothes on the hangers were all familiar to him. When he was certain the blue bag was not in the closet he trudged over and sat on her bed, trying to think of where it might be, but trapped in converging memories of the woman, the teasing, the quickly amorous smile, the saucy flaunt of skirt and hip. And how sometimes she was grave and sad, unmoved by his clowning. She had been a fragile-looking woman, because of her delicacy of feature, narrowness of waist, small-breasted figure. But she had been lithe and strong and fit. She disapproved of her own figure, deploring the breadth of hip, the heaviness of her thighs. Objectively he could see they were out of proportion on any perfectionist basis, but not as much as she believed, a sweet and hearty weight now lost forever, and he groaned aloud and startled himself with the sound of it in the silence of her room.

It did not take him long to satisfy himself that the bag was not in the apartment. There was no place left to search which could contain an object of that size. He was puzzled. Perhaps she had not felt right about it being hidden in the apartment and had taken it somewhere else. But had she done that, he was certain she would have asked him first. She had enjoyed letting him make decisions. She had told him many times he was the first man in her life of any force and authority, the first man to make her feel like a girl.

When he went out, Mrs. Carey was waiting, key in hand, her shrunken face pinched into a mask of churchly disapproval. "Took you long enough. Get what you were after?"

"Yes, thank you."

She gave the lock a decisive twist and said, "Old enough to be her paw, Sam Kimber."

"True enough, Martha."

"Can't count the times she never come home at all. Maybe she was with you every time. Maybe not. No fool like an old fool when it comes to prancing after a blonde head."

"Has anyone else been in the apartment since it happened?"

"Not unless they come with a key. I live in the front and this is in the back, and if I was to keep track of all comings and goings I wouldn't get my work done."

"Is that her key you have?"

"There's two to each apartment, good locks, and this is the spare. You tell Harv I want her key back, or I want the money to get a spare made."

"Did you see her at all yesterday?"

"From afar. We weren't never close. Seen her go by the corner walking back from Doc Nile's maybe some after noon, then scooting out in that car of hers at maybe half past. Wasn't to home night before last at all, come back in the early morning in a different outfit she wore leaving, so I guess she had some other place she was living too, but I guess you'd know more about that than me."

"I guess I would," Sam said and winked in a way that drew a shocked gasp from Martha Carey.

"Shameless!" she hissed.

He walked out and got into his big pale Chrysler. He drove slowly down Lemon Street, turning the air-conditioning to high, opening all the automatic windows for a moment to let the baked air escape. When he closed them again the car seemed to drift in an unreal silence through the dazzle of heat of early afternoon. He drove down through the center of the small city past the empty cars and the empty sidewalks and the bright glare of the store fronts. He hesitated as he neared the driveway to the parking lot behind his office, but then continued on. He went to the end of Citrus Avenue, drove around the small park past the Moorish arches of the public buildings and, several minutes later, realized he was out on the Brower Highway, passing the shopping centers and drive-ins, heading toward the place where she had died. Ten minutes from town he made his right turn. A half mile further he turned left into an overgrown sand road. Foliage brushed the side of the car and he drove three hundred yards through land he owned, down to the lake shore. It had always been known as Dayker's Lake until the promoter who developed the far shore engineered a name change to Flamingo Lake. He owned this half mile of lake front, untended, unimproved. He was glad to see no other cars parked there.

So, if she left the apartment at half past twelve, she would have arrived here at quarter to one, if she came directly

here. Parked where I am right now. Probably put her swim
suit on before she left the apartment. Wore that wrap-
around skirt thing over it. Got out. Tossed the skirt into the
car. Carried her stuff down to the little patch of sand. Towel,
beach bag, little radio. Settled herself. Then walked into the
water, tucking her hair into a swim cap. Three steps and
up to her waist, then deep.

He walked down to the sand. He wondered if he was
trying to punish himself. Did she yell for help? What
good did this do? He heard a motor sound and looked up
the shore line and saw a blue rowboat approaching, pro-
pelled by a small outboard motor. There were two young
boys in it, wiry and brown, their hair bleached almost white
by the sun. He heard one of them clearly over the chug
of the motor. "Right up there is where she drownded, right
out from where that guy is standing. And Jug didn't have
his tanks or nothing, just a mask and flippers and he found
her the second time down. He found her before those cops
ever even got the boat launched to drag for her. Right
about here, I think." The larger boy cut the motor off and
the boat slowed quickly. They stared at the water.

"How deep is it?" the smaller one asked.

"Jug says twenty feet."

"Was she down there a long time?"

"Long enough."

"How come that damn Jug got in on it anyways?"

"He saw all the people and come over and he had his
mask and flippers in the boat like he always has. It was
about two o'clock, I guess. I didn't even get to see her. But
I saw the ambulance leaving anyways."

"Jimmy, if she was alone, how come anybody knew she
drownded?"

"You're pretty stupid."

"Who says I'm stupid?"

"Some other people come to swim, see? And there's a car
parked and a towel and a little radio playing and everything,
and nobody around. They look around everywhere and get
nervous and start calling and nobody answers, and they
think maybe somebody has gone off in a boat, but there's no
sign of a boat and it had rained in the night and all they see
is bare foot prints going into the water. So somebody drove
back to the gas station and called the sheriff. And more people came flocking around. And Jug came over and found
her. They say she probably had a cramp."

Sam Kimber went slowly back to his car, backed around and drove away. It matched the report in the paper. Everything fitted fine. Except the small problem of a missing hundred and six thousand dollars. And no way to tell anybody it's missing. And somehow that makes the whole thing look wrong.

He drove back to town, parked behind his office building, unlocked the rear door and rode to the top floor in his small private elevator. It was a four story building he'd put up five years ago when he decided to leave the lonely house he'd built for Kitty. He'd had the Sam-Kim Construction Company put it up on Central Federal money, then lease the whole thing to Kimberland Enterprises on a long term lease, so Kimberland could turn around and sublease the two bottom floors. He'd worked a zoning exception so he could put his bachelor quarters and his private office on the top floor. The working staff of Kimberland Enterprises, Sam-Kim Construction and Kitty-Kim Groves and some of the other odds and ends worked on the third floor.

He went into his kitchen and opened a cold can of beer and stood at the window looking west toward Lake Larra. She'd lived out there in the Hanson place for a few short years with Kelsey Hanson. Along that shore of the lake it was a different kind of money. Solid old money, brought down out of solid old companies up north. Not my kind, he thought. Not the scrambling kind of money a lucky cracker boy can make if he comes out of the sloughs at the right time with a claw hammer, an old truck, a pocket full of nails and brass enough to believe his personal trend is up.

He realized he had forgotten lunch, so he ate a wedge of cheese and opened a second can of beer. A few more memories of her up here, because this wasn't out of bounds. She never rested quite easy in her mind about it, scrunching way down in the front seat driving in or out. The shack was best, way out at the end of noplace. She was most loving out there, most likely to be able to bring it about for herself out where there wasn't some part of her mind listening to sounds in the building.

With the beer in his hand he stalked through the living room, the big room that Lucille had said the pansy decorator from Orlando had made look like the lobby of an art movie house. As he pushed open the soundproofed door into the ante-office, he heard the busy clatter of the typewriter. It stopped abruptly as Angie Powell gave a great leap of surprise and put her hand to her throat. Mrs. Nimmits was at the corner table running a tabulator, and she said, "I swear, Mr. Sam, if you come through that door forty times a minute, Angie here would try to hop outen her skin every time."

"I didn't even know you were in there," Angie said accusingly.

Sam Kimber walked into his large office with Angie close at his heels, her hand full of notes. She closed the door behind her. He sat down, finished his beer and dropped the can in the wastebasket and said, "What new disasters we got today?"

As was her sometimes irritating habit, she gave him the least important messages first, pausing for instructions after each one, making memos to herself in her book. Angie Powell was six feet tall in flats, a big, glowing, earnest, pink and white girl in her early twenties with lavender eyes, large shiny teeth and dark golden curly hair. She was a superb swimmer, diver, bowler, water skier, tumbler, skater, dancer and secretary. And she was overpowering; there seemed to be so very much of her. She lived with a harridan mother and a father so tiny, so wispy, so self-effacing as to be almost invisible. She was an only child. She had worked for Sam for three years, the last two as his secretary, and she was entirely devoted, entirely loyal, full of good spirits but essentially humorless.

Long before he had become involved with Lucille, he had, in awe and out of curiosity, and perhaps like the climbers of mountains—because she was there—made a first and last valiant attempt to seduce her, making a reasonable excuse to get her into the adjoining quarters after overtime work. When he put his arms around her, she seemed to huddle and dwindle. And she began to shiver. He kissed her and it was like kissing a scared child. She looked at him, tears hanging on the lashes of the huge lavender eyes and said, "I can't smack you."

"What?"

"I don't know what to do. When boys try anything, I smack them a good one. Please let go, Mr. Sam."

He let go of her. "You always smack them?"

"I promised God and my mother I'd never do anything dirty in my whole life."

"Dirty!"

"I respectfully tender my resignation, Mr. Sam."

"What if we forget this happened and it never happens again?"

She thought it over. "Then I wouldn't want to resign, I guess."

Since that unwieldy episode he had learned, through observation and the most subtle of questions from time to time, that this big glowing girl had apparently never felt the slightest tremor of desire or curiosity in her life, and probably never would. She was the most implausible neuter in central Florida.

She came to the final note for his attention. "Gus Gable has been trying and trying to get hold of you, Mr. Sam."

"Tell him to come on over."

"From Jacksonville?"

"Oh, I didn't know he'd gone up there again. Get him on the phone if you can."

"First thing. He left three numbers to try the last time he called." She started to turn to leave and then said, "Mr. Sam?"

"Yes, Angie."

"I . . . I'm sorry about your friend."

"Thanks, Angie."

After she went out he wished, with a bitter amusement, he had given the blue bag to Angie. She would have hidden it, never opened it, never mentioned it. But, he wondered, why should I begin thinking of Lucille as less trustworthy? The choice was between the two of them, and Lucille was the brighter one, less likely to be tricked or trapped.

The phone rang and Gus was on the line. As usual he was so guarded as to be almost incomprehensible. "Sam, I got a call from one of our friends and it looked just good enough to make it worth while running up here, and I've had a pretty interesting day. I think I can safely say it's going to go our way, and the figure they're trying to clear right now is just ten thousand over my compromise guess. The field men are making a strong presentation, yes I can safely say a strong presentation to come up with that one as a final, and it goes across the right desk tomorrow, so I think I should be here in a position to give them a yes on that basis. It should be the first order of business, and all set by ten a.m."

"Nice going, Gus."

"But the flaw in the ointment could be the ninety days. It could get slashed down to sixty, which might make a squeeze."

"Accept sixty if that's the way they have to have it."

"That's the only weak part of the presentation the way I see it, and some new friends here agree with me. There's no hope of getting off a perpetual audit basis, and frankly I'd like to have it that way so we know where we stand from year to year, with every year filed away and closed so to speak."

"Suits me fine, boy."

"Say, a hell of a thing about Lucille. A hell of a thing and I felt actually and truly heartsick when I heard about it. A lovely little lady and a lot of laughs, and I extend my sympathy all the way down the line, Sam."

"Thanks, Gus."

"One of those things, I guess. One of the lumps in the road of life. We get this problem up here settled, and then you can go maybe on a cruise, get a change of scene and a new outlook."

"We'll see. You phone me tomorrow when you have the final word."

"I look on the black side of things, the blackest side you might say, but tomorrow I think I will give you good news, Sam. Goodby."

# Three

IN MAY the heat begins its five-month invasion of the flatlands and lake country of central Florida. There are breezes on the coasts, and summer tourists and packed beaches, but deep inland the country is emptied of all those who do not have to be there, and the survivors fortify themselves behind the busy rustle and clatter and cold clinical breath of the air-conditioning machines. It is a thick, wet, merciless, dispiriting heat, and those who endure it are like those who stay behind to guard a fortress, congratulating each other on their stamina, their sense of duty, and sneering at the ones who have fled. The high thunderstorms roll across the land, and after a brief illusion of coolness, everything settles back into the steamy silence. The insects and toads are in constant shrill chorus, and the birds make small random sounds. Tan fades because the direct sunlight is too much torment, and flesh is mottled with rash. People wrap a hand in a handkerchief before touching the door handle of a car. There is a stir of life in the early morning, and a mild resurgence after the sun goes down, but through the long days the streets of the small towns are a baking emptiness, the infrequent pedestrian moving slowly, his shoulders hunched against the weight of the sun, his eyes slitted against the unending glare. The owners of backyard swimming pools bring home cakes of ice to cool the pools to the point where it is possible to take an evening swim. Children are cross and often sick. Old friendships end abruptly.

But in May it is just beginning again, and all the other years are forgotten and there is a certain pleasure in the heat.

The funeral establishment of Crocker and Gain was rigorously air-conditioned to an impressive, sepulchral chill. But the vaulted downtown church was hot. The darkness of the interior gave no impression of coolness. It had been, Harv Walmo thought as he walked back to his office, like a badly lighted Turkish bath. Attending the church service had been an unnecessary gesture, he decided. Enough of the Hanson crowd around to make a good showing. And on top of that all the people who worked in one way or another for Sam Kimber. And then the ones who'd come out of curiosity. It would be a pretty sizeable stream of cars going out to the cemetery. If he hadn't attended, he would never have been missed. But then again, Sam might have noticed. And Sam was getting awfully edgy these days.

Sheriff Walmo walked with a slow dignity, his dark coat over his arm, his gray straw ranch hat set squarely on his large head.

When he arrived at his office, the man was waiting for him. Walmo had him wait another ten minutes and then had him sent in. He was a young man, tall, lithe, so heavy through the shoulders and neck as to give the impression of being or having been an athlete. He had such an olive tan and hair so black, Walmo wondered if he was Cuban. But under the dense black brows, the deep-set eyes were a clear, bright, inquisitive blue. He wore a light cord suit, a pale blue shirt, a dark blue bow tie. His manner and expression were guarded, but confident. And he waited to be asked to sit down.

"A courtesy call, Sheriff," he said. "My name is Paul Stanial. I'll be working in your area, with your permission. Here are my credentials."

Walmo looked at the cards. They showed that one Paul Stanial was licensed as a private investigator in the State of Florida and in Dade County, that he was employed by a Miami firm of a name familiar to Sheriff Walmo, that he had pistol permit number so and so.

"Well now," Harv Walmo said. "Well now, I guess this looks in order, and if'n it's some sort of civil action you're working on, you can tell me what it is and go on ahead about your business and I appreciate your stopping in. But if it's some kind of criminal matter, our policy is work with you so there's no confusion going on."

"I've been employed to conduct a quiet investigation to determine if any criminal action has taken place," Stanial said carefully. "If at any time during my investigation I turn up anything which would indicate such a criminal action has taken place, I shall turn that information over to you. I intend to check in with the city police department also, of course."

"Now we maybe aren't perfect around here, Mr. Stanial, but it would surprise me if we missed out on anything going on that's big enough to warrant sending a man up here from Miami. This here is a mighty clean county. So what criminal act is supposed to took place?"

"The client wishes to be assured that the death of Mrs. Kelsey Hanson was not murder."

Walmo's thick jaw sagged. "Murder! By God that poor girl drowned!"

Stanial smiled briefly. "Without help. That's the point, I guess."

"Now you can't come in here and get people all stirred up over . . ."

"Sheriff, I don't want publicity any more than you do. This will be a quiet investigation. It was an accidental death, apparently. I have a cover story I don't believe anyone will question." He handed a letter and a calling card to the Sheriff. The card identified Stanial as a claims adjustor for a New England life insurance company, and the letter was a form request for an investigation and report on the death of Lucille Larrimore Hanson in connection with policy number so and so dated so and so in the amount of $25,000—said form letter having been apparently sent from the home office to the Miami field office.

"I . . . guess that'll work all right," Walmo said hesitantly. "I plan to tell the people I talk to that it has a double indemnity provision which is voided by suicide. That gives me a chance to ask more personal questions."

"It wasn't murder and it wasn't suicide."

"Perhaps that's what we'll tell the client after the investigation is complete. But we've been hired to do it."

"Somebody is throwing their money down a hole. Who?"

Stanial bit his lip for a moment. "The courts have upheld my right not to disclose that information, Sheriff, but I usually play it by ear. In this case I see no harm in telling you. We've been employed by the dead woman's sister—a Miss Barbara Larrimore."

"The sister? The one come down for the funeral?"

"Yes. I haven't seen her yet, though."

"Now what would put such a crazy idea into her head and make her waste her money like this?"

"I have no idea," Stanial said.

Walmo stared skeptically at the younger man for a few moments. "You said something about turning any evidence over if you find any, which you won't. You able to recognize legal evidence if you happen to trip over it?"

Stanial looked at Walmo so bleakly that Walmo hastily revised Stanial's estimated age, adding four or five years. "I had graduate training, CIC work, and six years as a professional officer of the law, Sheriff."

"Why'd you quit?"

"Is it important?"

"Just a friendly question."

"It was a big northern city, Sheriff, with a force rated tops by the FBI. So the voters changed the city charter, and then the politicians cleaned out the top ranks of professional cops, filled the jobs with courthouse slobs, and the whole structure collapsed in less than a year. I've been in this work two years. I was transferred to Miami four months ago. I'd rather be wearing a badge, but I can assure you that I know the rules of evidence and I know proper police procedure, and I know from reading the newspaper accounts that you can't prove beyond doubt that woman was alone when she drowned."

"It was just a friendly question," Walmo said.

Stanial smiled, and it seemed to Walmo an exceptionally warm and likeable smile for a man who had looked so icy a moment before. "If it's just hysteria, I'll try to wrap it up fast enough to keep the fee down. To start me off, Sheriff, who were the three people closest to Mrs. Hanson?"

"The three? Her husband. And she worked for Doc Nile. And there's Sam Kimber . . . a good friend."

"If you haven't got time right now I can come back, Sheriff. But I would like to hear a little about those three people."

Walmo leaned back. "I've got the time, son. All the time we need."


Barbara Larrimore was glad to get back to the Orangeland Motel after the final part of funeral protocol, that brief graveside ceremony. The church service had begun at two and she was back at the motel by three thirty. She hastened out of her dark, damp, heavy clothing, aimed the air-conditioner vents toward the bed, took off every stitch and stretched out gratefully.

She hoped she had not offended the Yateses, Jason and Bonny. But they had been so very insistent that she should leave the motel and come out to their lakeside home. They said she could have the whole guest wing to herself. And Kelsey Hanson seemed to think it a good idea too. "I'll help you pack, dear, and Jase can check you out," the blonde woman said. Finally she had to be almost rude before they gave up and went away and left her there alone.

She remembered Lucille's savage comments about Kelsey's group of friends in one of the letters she wrote after she and Kelsey had separated. "They are very pretty people, and so terribly cordial and generous and open and well-mannered. They smother you with warm welcomes, and they all seem to look at you, man and woman, with the same fond wish to like you and be liked. They have a good deal of money and what I suppose you would call on the surface the gracious life. The men do a little, not very much, just enough so they appear to have offices to go to, or things to manage. They have a lot of little inside jokes and sayings, and they all tell hilarious anecdotes and tell them very well. And as you are beginning to think these are the world's finest, they begin to change. Or maybe you begin to notice things. I don't know. Underneath their pretty faces is a total and vulgar preoccupation with who got how drunk and when and where, and who screwed whom. Maybe it's just boredom using up trivial people, but I found them wicked. And Kelsey is one of them, to the core. Is wicked too ancient and biblical a word, Barb? I am not a prude. Maybe a certain amount of dignity is my problem. I have a careful desire to be able to re-

member what I said and to whom, and who did what to me.
There are nice people here, as there are everywhere, and
probably there are little groups like this in Hartford and
Plattsburg. But this is Kelsey's way of life, not mine, and
our separation is mostly due, I guess, to his unspoken attitude that, in time, I could get used to it. Now, just a few
weeks away from it all, it has become unreal somehow."

It was a splendid word, Barbara thought. Unreal. Unreal
not to see or hear any slightest reference to the fact Lucille and Kelsey had been living apart for almost a year. They
all acted as though Lucille had died of an accident while on
a short trip, a reluctant separation from her loving young
husband. And it would have been unthinkable to suggest she
not be buried in the Hanson plot. She was still married to a
Hanson. And Kelsey's grief was unmistakably genuine. He
was like a man stunned. He looked as if his head had been
boiled over a slow fire. His movements were uncertain. He
was, undeniably, a man bereft.

An additional unreality was the absence of blood relatives.
She was used to great throngs of relatives at funerals. But,
according to the lengthy and rather stilted radio message of
sympathy from the elder Hansons, their ship was five days
out of Bombay when they received the message. Kelsey was
an only child. There were cousins in California, and that was
all. And too far for the Larrimores to come, she thought.

With comfort and coolness came the energy to make the
necessary phone call. It went through immediately and her
Aunt Jen answered.

"How was the service, dear?"

"Is Mother asleep?"

A frail familiar voice came on the line. "I heard it ring,
dear, and I thought it might be you so I'm on the bedroom
phone."

"How are you feeling, Mom?"

"Pretty well, I guess. Considering. How was the service?"

"Really beautiful. A big church and lots of flowers, and it
was really packed."

"Lucille was always a very popular girl," Aunt Jen said.

"How did my poor darling look?" Mrs. Larrimore asked.
"Did you get a chance to see her?"

"This morning, right after I got in, Mom. She looked very
peaceful."

"Those people always put too much make-up on."

"They didn't do that to Lu, really."

"Is it a pretty cemetery, dear?"

"It's in sort of rolling country and very well kept. The Hanson plot is right near a great big live oak tree, with Spanish moss."

She heard heartbreak sounds, and Aunt Jen said, "You hold on just a minute, Barbie." In a few minutes Aunt Jen came back and said, "I made her hang up. She's really pretty weak today, and she's had about all she can take. She'll want to know about who was there, and how many cars and what kind of flowers and what kind of a casket and all that, and what poor Lu was buried in, and what happens to her things and so on, but I don't want to take time on that now because I want to get back to her. So put it all in a letter and get it in the mail tonight, dear. And then you hurry on back home."

"Aunt Jen, I might have to stay a few days."

"Why, child?"

"There's some sort of legal things."

"But can't you tell some local lawyer to handle those things?"

"I have to know what they are before I can tell him how to handle them, don't I?"

"Shouldn't things like that be up to your mother and me?"

"Aunt Jen, I'm not a child and I'm not an idiot. I'm twenty-five years old and I think you can credit me with some sense of responsibility."

"You sound like a snip."

"I might have to stay a few days. I *will* let you know, and I *will* come home as soon as I can. And . . . none of this is easy."

"I know, child. I didn't mean to be grouchy."

After she hung up she stretched out again, knowing she would soon have to make the effort and take a shower. She hoped she had sounded more assured than she felt. The lie about legal things was flimsy. She wondered how Aunt Jen and her mother would react were they to know the real reason why she wanted to stay a few days. But it was impossible to subject them to that, when it might turn out false after all. It was horrid enough losing Lu without having to wonder if someone had killed her. If it was proven, they would have to know, of course.

She was wise enough about herself to know that the suspicion of murder, ugly as it seemed, had helped sustain her throughout this incredible day of sacred words and burial.

Somehow, were it pure accident, it made the world a non-sensical place. Lucille had deserved so much more, and had sounded in her letters as if she could be on the verge of finding it.

Such an unreal day, riding in the back seat of the limousine with Kelsey Hanson, the two of them and a driver, the first car after the hearse, riding behind Lucille with the silent, suffering, estranged husband, through the hot glare of streets, where a few people stopped and stared.

And the sudden geographical spasm made loss more endurable through making it less easy to comprehend. She had been taken from the narrow grubby orderly Maytime of Boston, held suspended in the placid jet over a pastel earth slowly turning, then pulled down into this rank and muggy place where the pretty people, under their tin palm fronds, buried her only sister and kept looking at her without anxiety as though to say, "See how nicely we do it?"

She had finished her shower and she was tucking her thin white blouse into her dark skirt when there was a knock at her door. She went to the door and leaned close to it and asked who it was.

"Stanial," the voice said.

"Just a moment please." She stepped into her sandals, yanked a brush through her lively wiry brown hair, slashed her mouth quickly with lipstick, patted the bed smooth, dropped random clothing into the big bottom drawer of the bureau and let him in, performing all these actions without pause or hesitation, moving from one into the next with a balance and coordination that made it all a brief segment of a strange realistic dance.

He was against the outside glare and she could not see him clearly until he was inside and the door was closed. And then she could not feel the confidence she had hoped to feel. He looked too ordinary. Just a rather bland youngish man of dark complexion, too carefully dressed for the climate and the area. As they met each other for the first time, shook hands rather stiffly, she thought, He could be coming to make an estimate. But not to sell anything, because he makes no attempt to be ingratiating. A man who comes to collect, or make out a form, and isn't particularly interested because the account is so small. The only thing not quite ordinary about him was an impression of physical durability, not so much because of the heft of his shoulders as the deft and positive way he moved.

There were two chairs. She brought the straight chair over from the desk and they sat by the window, facing each other across the lamp table.

"It might be nothing at all," she said.

"It might be nothing, and it might be something, and we'll satisfy ourselves one way or the other, Miss Larrimore."

"Did you bring the letter?"

He took it out of his inside jacket pocket. "You can have it back. I have a photocopy."

"Did you think that part of it sounded . . . strange?"

"Yes."

But his tone was so noncommittal she had to open the letter and look at the strange part again to reassure herself. The letter had arrived the same day as the news she was dead.

The odd part read, "Problems, problems, problems. This is a strange one all tangled up into emotions and ethics and a couple of kinds of secrecy. I'm trying to sort it out and decide what to do. You seem to be my only outlet on some things, kid sister, so bear with me. The details later. I was very slickly trapped into betraying a confidence, and too much of a coward—as yet—to tell the person who trusted me that the secret is out. Not all the way, but enough to make me uneasy. Now a third person has entered the picture, and strangely enough so that, for the first time, I can believe I might actually be in some sort of danger. Nothing specific. Just a crinkly feeling at the back of the neck. Something of value is involved, of course. What else makes people sly and dangerous? I can take some sly little steps of my own to put B and C off the scent, or just tell A the whole thing, or do both in that order, which might make me look less of an idiot. Sorry to inflict the Ian Fleming bit, Barb, but you'll get the whole story after it's over."

Barbara looked defiantly at Paul Stanial. "It *is* enough, dammit! Lu was like a fish in the water. Cramps drown people because they panic."

"Her lungs were full of water and there wasn't a mark on her."

"Investigation over?"

She became uncomfortably aware of the compulsive impact of those very blue deep-set eyes, and before she looked away she thought she saw amusement.

"I can give it the television treatment if you'd be more at home with that, Miss Larrimore." He deepened his voice. "By

God, little lady, this is more than coincidence, or my name ain't Private Eye Maloney." In his normal tone he said, "Or we can deal with facts. And when we can connect several facts with a supposition, we can check out the supposition."

"Please. I'm sorry."

"It's hardly ever dramatic, Miss Larrimore. People hear about the dramatic ones and they remember the dramatic ones. And for everyone like that, there's a thousand little dirty ones nobody remembers. And lots of times there's nothing at all. You wait and watch and talk and think and you end up with nothing at all. You have to know that." For a moment his poise was uncertain. "You're another fact, you know."

"How?"

"Complaints are rated by the people who make them. You seem like an organized person. Was your sister, too?"

"Organized? She was a very stable person, Mr. Stanial. She didn't exaggerate things or create mysteries. Neither do I."

"So the letter is more valid and the complaint is more valid. Do you follow me?"

"I think so."

"A little background would help. On both of you."

"The Larrimore girls," she said with a trace of bitterness, taking the proffered cigarette, leaning to the light. "She was the pretty one. The proper social standing, but not the money. Oh, little bits came in, decently inherited from great-uncles and so on, enough to make the college thing a little bit less of a scramble, but still a scramble. Daddy died when we were small, right in the midst of a business gamble which might have worked out if he'd lived. Mother is the sort of woman who would never marry again. So there was reluctant charity from both sides of the family, always called something else. And an old apartment on the wrong end of a good street. Mother collapsed and Daddy's maiden sister, Aunt Jen, came to hold it all together temporarily. She found the apartment, got us moved and has stayed with us ever since. I don't want to sound like something out of Henry James, but genteel poverty is the worst kind, I think, because you have to keep imitating the standards you are supposed to live up to. Break one cup of the good tea service and it is a disaster, believe me. And one is always changing hems and necklines and dying things this season's color, and scrounging up dues for something you can't afford not to belong to because you'll lose the contacts. Four females in an apartment, Mr. Stanial. It's a stale life.

"Lu fulfilled the quota. Kelsey was very charming and very decorative and very rich, in a background way. It was a lovely little wedding, and it damned near cleaned us out. But we made it. And then, as it turned out, we hadn't made it at all. I brought Lu's letters, just in case. I squirrel things away. String, letters, stamps with the stickum gone. Mother has congestive heart disease, and she can last six months or six years. I work in a brokerage office. I go to work and I come home. I could be twenty-five or fifty-five and it wouldn't seem to make much difference. . . ." She stopped abruptly and looked at him with a startled expression. "I don't go on like this to people. It's the crazy day and the crazy heat and the trip." She stabbed her cigarette out in the shallow ashtray and was suddenly afraid she was going to start crying, so she stood up and moved away from him.

"The letters would be a help, Barbara."

"Don't patronize me!"

"Don't keep your guard so high. We'll be working on this thing for a little while. Paul and Barbara is easier. Also, it helps me. You'll talk a little more freely as Barbara."

She whirled and stared at him. "More freely than just now? No thanks. I worked myself into a nice case of self-pity, and it's a lousy emotion. Not tears for my sister. Tears for me."

"How about the letters?"

She got them out of the pocket of her suitcase and took them to him and sat near him again. "It's sort of a . . . representative collection. The office letters, I guess you can call them. She'd write just the normal sort of things to me at home, or to mother mostly. The . . . very personal ones came to the office, Paul."

"Don't be so uncertain, Barbara. My role is personal and confidential, and this is the death of a woman, and her emotional life is pertinent."

He held his hand out and she gave him the packet of letters. "I don't see how you can just go around and find out anything from all these people here."

He explained his cover and showed her the insurance identifications which had been prepared for him. She understood much more quickly than Walmo had, saying, with approval, "And they all think you're trying to prove suicide to save money for your company. Paul, will my staying here a few days spoil anything? Will anybody think anything is funny if you see me and talk to me?"

He shrugged. "It will help, if anything. You and your mother are beneficiaries under this imaginary policy, and you're indignant about this investigation and hang around to make sure I don't cheat you. This sort of thing is standard procedure, actually. You have to give people a story they will understand and accept, and then they talk."

She studied him. "So I guess you should look sort of ordinary." She flushed. "I just meant that . . ."

"You try to look like what you're supposed to be. It helps."

Knowing it sounded trivial, but unable to help herself, she said, "I guess it must be very interesting work."

His whole face and manner seemed to change, and he did not look ordinary at all. There was a look of black and bitter forces just below the surface of this man, a wretchedness and a fury that startled her at the same time as it intrigued her. And just as suddenly he forced himself back to blandness. "Sometimes," he said. "Now, can I ask you how much of this you can afford?"

"I sneaked a thousand dollars out of a trust thing, fifteen hundred actually, a thousand for this. The Boston office explained to me that it won't . . . last very long. I was thinking a thousand dollars might be enough, but now I guess it might not, really. Five hundred for the trip and all. I've got my ticket back, and I can take the time off charged to my vacation. And money to stay here a while."

He lost some of his poise again, and it made him look younger. "I want to tell you one thing. It's sort of iffy, but it's something you should understand. Because if you understand it in advance and have time to think about it, then there's less chance of you doing something foolish *if* it comes up."

"What in the world . . ."

The blue stare was cold and direct. "Law is a power equation, Barbara. Think of the things in a criminal case as a kind of a chain. The links are called accumulating evidence, proving motive, booking and charging, grand jury indictment, trial, conviction, sentence, appeal, confirmation, punishment. Money and power are like big nippers. They can open any link at any portion of the chain and the whole thing is over. Big local names in this, Barbara. Hanson. Kimber. So don't be idealistic. I might be able to get the raw material for a pretty good file and turn it over to the authorities and have it sag into nothing. It would have to be a perfect file, unless it's against sombody of no importance. And this power thing works more effectively in semi-rural areas like this one. There'll be no fearless officials and no valiant newspaper to rally to the cause of eternal justice. Too much give and take is involved. It isn't the best of all possible worlds, but it's the best we have, and we've nailed some big ones."

"Are you trying to tell me that you might find out who killed my sister and still not be able to . . ."

"We might come up with a reasonable certainty, and it wouldn't be enough. And you might have to live with it, knowing X is down here, fat and happy and unpunished. *Could* you live with it?"

"Why, I would shout it from the housetops and . . ."

"Do time for criminal slander, or get grabbed and committed to a mental institution. Barbara, we either play this cold and go as far as we can and then quit and drop it, or we don't start it at all."

She looked down for a long time and then gave a small jerky nod. She looked up at him with a wan smile. "The education of Barbara Larrimore," she said.

"I'm sorry you have to find out these things this way."

"Will I be able to help you in any way?"

"It might be possible. I just don't know what will open up."

"Are you going to read the letters now?"

"I'll go over them tonight. By the way, I checked in here, too. I'm on the other side, in the back. Unit 51." He glanced at his watch and stood up. "I've got an appointment to see Doctor Nile. Do you have a car?"

"No. This is so close in. Just three or four blocks to the middle of town."

"And people looking at you and telling each other who you are, and the bold ones coming over to extend sympathy? Are you ready for that?"

"I was . . . wondering about it."

"Why don't you try to take a nap? I'll pick you up sometime after six and we'll go eat over in Leesburg or Ocala. They're both about thirty or forty minutes away." He smiled. "And the mileage won't go on my voucher. Sound all right to you?"

"Yes it does, Paul. Thank you."

# Four

DOCTOR RUFUS NILE was a short man of fifty, plump but without any suggestion of softness. He was a rubbery, darting, bouncing little man, pink and scrubbed and starched. He had an Einstein shock of gray hair, eyes a-goggle behind thick corrective lenses, a wide range of explosive conversational tricks, expressions, gestures—puffing his cheeks, smacking his lips, rolling his eyes, slapping, patting, thumping himself for all the world, Stanial thought, like a little kid who has to go, and translates discomfort into random energy.

As a new floor covering was being put down in Nile's office, they met in one of his treatment rooms, and during the first few minutes Stanial found himself making continual reappraisals of the little man. At first he thought him a clown striving for laughs. Then he wondered if perhaps Rufus Nile was a totally humorless man. His final appraisal was that this was a complex and, quite possibly, a shy man who had manufactured a public image to hide behind. The humor was there, but it was of a cold variety directed more subtly than any clown motions could be.

Particularly disconcerting was Nile's habit of asking a question, then abruptly tilting his head, shoving it forward, assuming a totally vacuous expression and following the question up with an insistent, "Hah?"

"Did she seem troubled the last few weeks, Doctor?"

"Troubled? How are you orienting this, Stanial? You want me to say depressed? Hah? No, my boy. You're reaching too far, too far. I was fond of Lucille. Fond or not, I keep a close watch on my personnel. Doctors' offices have a massive turnover, and you like to guess when you're going to lose the next one. Never lost one this way though."

"Did you think you were going to lose her?"

"A woman like that? Hah? Eventually. She was marking time. Had the blessed sense to walk out on that Hanson pup. And agree to a one-year cooling-off period. So I knew I'd lose her at the end of a year."

"Was she disturbed at the failure of her marriage?"

"What do you think? Hah? A woman like that? Marriage

39

wasn't a casual thing. Certainly disturbed. Upset. Sense of failure. It troubled her. That's the word we started with. And she got involved with Sam Kimber. That troubled her too. I'm no moralist, Stanial. We all get into conflict with our own standards for ourselves, if we're worth a damn. She was. The Sam Kimber thing surprised a lot of people, mostly the ones that take him at face value. Known Sam a long time. More complex than he lets on. God knows how it got started between them. Unlikely, sort of. And they kept it discreet. But a place this size, they weren't about to keep it a secret. After Kitty Kimber died, Sam never took up with anybody. There were plenty of them who made the attempt. Sam did his prowling other places. And not often, I'd say. Anyway, I guess Lucille didn't have an image of herself as a woman who'd get into that kind of a situation. A quiet woman, pretty and sort of cool and careful looking. But a good healthy female creature in the best part of her life. Pretty much alone and vulnerable and far from home. She was starting to turn a little brittle and precise. And Sam turned her back into a woman. My guess, it startled her considerable to find out she could get into a relationship as physical as that. I'd guess Sam brought her alive more than marriage ever did. All this isn't any of my business, and it isn't any of yours or any of the North Atlantic Mutual Life's, but when you start hinting around about suicide it seems to me it's time I tell you the reasons why the idea doesn't fit. If she was feeling guilt, which I don't doubt, it was less than the contentment. She'd come to work some mornings in a dream, slow and soft and misty, and dark circles around her eyes and a little Mona Lisa smile on her, and as a practicing physician I can say that maybe one woman in ten has the combination of glands and good luck and plain sensual capacity to get herself into that kind of condition. And it doesn't exactly lead to a suicidal mood, Stanial, because it's a celebration of the sweetness of life, and just as far from death as you can get."

"But how about the last few weeks?"

"Now you want to take the usual suicide motives one by one? Hah? My people get a physical whenever there's any halfway excuse for it, and last month I had the excuse with Lucille because she was over a week late and nervous about it and she wanted a rabbit test. It was negative, and she came around the next day or so. And if it hadn't been negative, she wouldn't have wanted anything done because that wasn't her style. Gave her a complete check. So damned healthy she had enough vitality for three women. Sam hadn't changed, so that part of her life hadn't gone wrong. From her pay and the support from Kelse Hanson and some little investment, she had enough over so she was sending her mother a little every month. Rule out money. That marriage was dead and going to stay dead, because not only had she found out the difference between a man and a boy, Hanson wasn't trying any kind of selling job on her. Too busy trying to crawl back into the college-boy role, like the first step in working his way back to the womb. Had my own guess about it. When the year was up she'd put in for the divorce and head north, and Sam would find out then what she was worth to him and go marry her and bring her back, but a man like Sam isn't going to marry until he finds out, like a shot in the head, he can't do without it."

"Doctor, you keep side-stepping."

"Give me a chance. Now how about momentary mental instability? Nothing neurotic about Lucille. Solid as a rock. These past few weeks? Hah? So I'll say she had something on her mind. But I don't know what it was."

"But you could make a guess?"

Rufus Nile hopped down off the treatment table, yanked a drawer open, took out an opened bottle of Jack Daniels, held it up and said, "Hah?"

"With plain water, thanks."

"End of the day." He fixed the drinks in large paper cups. "Got a weakness for guessing. Take the situation with Sam. He doesn't go around telling anybody anything without a reason. He made it awful damn fast. Honesty is relative. So here you have this intense physical affair going on. And she has standards set pretty high, in spite of the affair. For a woman like that it has to be something significant. Some kind of love. She never knew anybody like Sam Kimber before. Now just suppose she found out, as Sam got more chummy with her, that in a business way he was playing it so close to the line, you could flip a coin to find out whether to call him crooked or not? It's just the sort of thing that would worry a woman like that in just the way she seemed worried. She'd know you can't change a man like Sam. So it would trouble her. She'd wonder if that made the relationship a little more unsanitary. Understand, I'm only guessing. But there are people around who could have told her a few stories about Sam. And they wouldn't sound pretty. But it isn't anything she'd kill herself over. She might decide to start untangling herself, or she might decide the hell with it, but there wouldn't be room for any third decision. I know if you can save your company that twenty-five thousand, you'll be a big man and get a bonus maybe, but it wouldn't be fair and it wouldn't be reasonable."

"But she was a very good swimmer."

"And it was about ninety-three in the shade and that lake always runs a little colder than the others. It can happen to the best. Abdominal cramps maybe, jacknifed her right up. Don't suicides leave notes?"

"Not when they know what it will do to the insurance, Doctor."

Nile shook his head quickly. "Stanial, you'll make a good try at it, but you won't make it stick."

Watching Nile obliquely and carefully, Stanial said in a joking tone, "Maybe I'd be better off if there was a murder clause, too."

"It would make more sense than suicide?"

"Would it?"

"Now hold on!" Nile said angrily. "I said no word about murder. I was just trying to say suicide is the most unlikely thing I can think of."

Stanial leaned against the window sill sipping his drink. As a professional he had learned long ago to divide the people he interrogated into his own categories, based on his own value judgments. Curiously, the most basic dividing line seemed to be based on self-awareness and self-respect. Without regard to lines of social or financial or educational demarcation, some people seemed to fit easily inside their skins, to be at home with themselves. They could be car washers or bank presidents, but they—like this Doctor Nile —made the whole thing easier by having no aching need to exaggerate or diminish their own importance in his eyes. They said what they believed rather than what they thought you wanted them to believe. So you could sort out what they said, knowing the significant things were indeed significant, not merely attempts to get attention or to avoid attention. When they lied, the motives were usually obvious and understandable. The ones not at home with themselves were difficult. They believed the world had judged them wrongly, when in fact they had made the faulty appraisal. And, bank president or car washer, they had in small doses those diseases the psychiatrists put names to—a fragment of neurosis, a crumb of paranoia, a taint of the psychotic. At the same time as they misled themselves, for reasons never obvious, they were also misleading you, because their vision of reality was flawed. You could not like them because in a very basic way they did not like themselves. But it was easy to like the Doc Niles of the world. It was something you had to sense. There were no rules. There was only practice.

"Is accident more likely than murder?"

"Certainly! Who'd kill Lucille?"

Stanial gave Nile his most disarming grin. "Let's see. You, because you'd fallen in love with her and couldn't stand the thought of her seeing Sam Kimber all the time. Hanson, because he knew she'd refuse to come back to him at the end of the year. Sam Kimber, because he told her too much about his business affairs and she threatened to turn him in. Or somebody who wanted her out of the way so they'd have the inside track with Sam. Or some drunk who happened along."

"Hell, boy, you got imaginitis. That's an acute inflamation of the imagination."

"It's a reaction to too many dull insurance cases. I get one with a beautiful woman involved, I lose control."

"Or it could be Martha Carey, her landlady, striking a blow for chastity. Or one of Hanson's college girls, making sure the marriage wouldn't pick up again where it left off. Or one of Hanson's pals who got turned down by Lucille and couldn't stand the shame of it. Hah?"

"You do pretty good too, Doctor."

"Any number can play. But it was an accident. One hell of a lot of people drown in Florida every year. They have a knack for it, seems like. There's so damn much water, they lose respect for it. The times it makes you sick are the toddlers, whole platoons of them, that fall into the ponds and the lakes and the drainage ditches and the swimming pools. Somebody took their eye off the kid for thirty seconds. Had one last month. Two years old. Brought him around but he'd been out so long the brain damage was severe. Died of pneumonia on the fifth day. Probably just as well."

"Did you examine Lucille's body?"

"I'm not the coroner. That's Bert Dell. He's got better political connections, but he's a good man. From the degree of cyanosis it was drowning beyond a doubt, and he estimated she was under for at least thirty minutes before they brought her up. Billy Gain had himself a time bleaching out that blue so they could leave the box open. Goddam barbaric custom."

"Agreed."

"An essential dignity to death. Hah? What kind of veneration is it to pretty up the husk? Another little remedy for pain and sorrow, Stanial?"

"A light one, thanks."

"Can you fold your tent now, or are you going to keep talking to people?"

"I couldn't sell the company on doing less than five interviews, and then I'll have to talk to some of the people who were on the scene so I can make a detailed report. And I've got the younger sister in my hair."

"Saw her at the service, not to speak to. Nice-looking girl."

"She's afraid the company'll try to put something over on her. I can't seem to make her believe we won't stoop to faking anything."

"You'll talk to Sam Kimber?"

"Have to."

Nile puffed his cheeks and patted his sturdy belly. "Word of advice, boy. Play it very very straight with Sam. You got a little tricky with me here and there, and that's your job, I suppose. But just because Sam might look and act a little bit country-boy, don't rate him low. He'd smile and look a little sleepy if you get cute with him, and it wouldn't get you a thing. And ten minutes later he'd pick up the phone and make a call or two, and you'd be looking for work."

"Thanks for the warning."

"He's like an old 'gator. On the mud bank they look as if they're smiling. That's because they've got meat tucked away in the bottom of the pond, getting ripe."

"How about Hanson?"

"There's not a thing he can do for you or to you, except maybe try to punch you in the mouth if he's drinking. And from the look of you, that would be a mistake. Never mess with a man who looks a couple of inches shorter than he is. I'd guess you at one-sixty if that didn't look like an eighteen neck size."

"Seventeen and a half. One ninety-three."

"Wrestler?"

"And the weights and the bars and the rings. Fun at the time, but I'm paying for it now, because I have to work out or it turns to flab. Thanks for the drink and thanks for the talk, Doctor."

"You have not called me Doc. And you haven't asked for any free advice. So come around any weekday the same time and rap on the back door. This is the pause in the day's occupation that is known as the Daniels' hour. Bad luck on your mission, but good luck to you, boy."

"Thank you, Doctor. I don't want to step on any toes. There are towns where people don't like questions of any kind about anything."

"No trouble here, Stanial. It's a—what would you call it? —fragmented society. In one way or another, except for some of the oldest families out along Lake Larra, and a few old ones in town and some of the grove money, everybody is a come-lately. It's growing fast and changing fast. Not for the better. County population twice what it was ten years ago. The lines are vague. I guess there aren't any towns any more the way there used to be. Just shopping centers with houses around them."

Barbara Larrimore was quiet when he picked her up and walked her out to his dark little utilitarian two-door sedan. In the evening angle of the sun he saw that her eyes were puffy, the lids reddened, her lips swollen.

"Have a nap?" he asked as they drove away.

"A little one. I . . . didn't think I was going to cry so soon. I thought it would come later. But after you left me I was thinking . . . off guard, I guess . . . how I'd tell Lu about all this. So much to tell her. And then all of a sudden I knew . . . I *really* knew . . . I'd never be able to tell her anything, ever again. The terrible finality of it hit me, I guess for the first time. And now it isn't real again. It's gone away for now, but it'll come back again I guess."

"That's the way it happens. Will Ocala be all right?"

"Anything you say. Have you lost anybody that close to you, Paul?"

"I've made a career of it."

"Oh?"

"I'm sorry. That sounded pretty smart. My parents are alive. In Michigan. I lost an older brother. He was the hero. I couldn't do things right. I wanted to be able to do them right and get him to finally approve of me. And when I started to be able to do a few things right, then he wasn't around. But when anything does work out and I feel good about it, there's a little sort of flash in my mind. Sort of

'How about this, Joe?' And then I feel the loss. He was one of the most physically powerful people I've ever seen. And I tried to toughen myself up to his standards when I was a kid. I guess I'm still looking for his approval. And I lost a wife too—not in the same way, but as completely. And that gives you a funny feeling. If Janey was dead, then there would be that finality you mentioned. I mean a finality you can't argue with. But she's alive and in Texas. In the Hill Country. Kerrville. I know there'll never be any contact with her ever again. But she's still in the world, and I dream sometimes about seeing her, but when I wake up I know it's the last damn thing I want to do."

"Are you talking like this to help me?"

"Or myself. I don't know, Barbara."

"I shouldn't have said that. It makes it harder to talk. For both of us. I should have just let it happen. Tell me about Janey."

"It isn't dramatic at all. Her people made her feel that she was very very precious and unique. And she had lessons in everything you can possibly teach a kid. And so her people thought it was a hell of a waste to throw it all away on a cop. Like in a primitive tribe, she'd have been the one worth the most head of cattle. But she didn't seem to think that way. And if we'd had children, she might have stayed too busy to notice. Or gotten a job that would have been demanding. I guess she got the feeling after awhile life wasn't making much use of her. When she wanted out, I let her go. What can you do? She was plain bored, and it made her irritable and sad. Now she has the big house and the entertainment and the kids and a hand in running some kind of an angora goat ranch. Everybody always liked her."

"She didn't love you."

"That was the thing they didn't give her any lessons in. She'd tell you she did, and believe it. And tell you that now she loves this Texan. But I don't know. Maybe if any person has absolute self-confidence, they can't really love anybody else."

She laughed abruptly. "That isn't my problem."

After he had passed a slower car he looked over at her. When he had first met her he had mistaken her habitual expression for one of petulance, of a kind of permanent sulkiness. But now it seemed to him that the small frown lines and the set of her mouth indicated a resolute endurance. The sun was almost gone and she squinted ahead into the light, her head thrust forward, her hands placid in her lap. Her hair was a glossy brown with paler highlights, her forehead high, her eyes green-gray, her face a long oval, slightly plump. She had called Lucille the pretty sister, and from the pictures he had been given of Lucille, there was a conditional accuracy to that statement. This younger woman was attractive in her own way, less obvious. Her long round arms and legs and a kind of placidity of her body in repose gave an impression of indolence, of low vital forces, yet she moved with a deft swiftness at any small task. In the first talk with her he had thought her rather neutral, without sensual impact. But in the car with her now, he began to sense his own awareness of her, to see in the placement of an ear, hinge of the wrist, roundness of knee, those gentle perfections which eluded a hasty scrutiny.

By the time they were half-finished with dinner he knew she had recovered enough of her normal spirit to be told of the interrogation of Doctor Nile. He found himself describing Nile in ways that would make her laugh. But she sobered when he told her of Nile's guess as to why Lucille had seemed troubled during the past few weeks.

"It fits the letter," Barbara said. "Mr. Kimber trusted her with some kind of secret, and then she was trapped into telling somebody else. And maybe the *kind* of secret was bothering her—I mean if Mr. Kimber explained it one way and she found out there was some other way to explain it. . . . It gets vague doesn't it."

"There's a lot more people to talk to."

"But how can you find out what the secret was?"

"Maybe it will be a case of finding out what it wasn't. Like a crossword puzzle. Once you get one or two letters of the key word, the number of possibilities are reduced."

"She was killed, Paul," Barbara said in a strange tone. "She came down here and they killed her." The tears came with no warning. She buried her face in her hands. She went to the rest room. She was gone ten minutes. She came back and slid into the booth opposite him and said, "I'm sorry."

"It's all right."

"Can you give me something to do tomorrow? I'll be better if I have something to do."

"I'll find something."

"Please don't patronize me."

"I'll find something. I haven't gone far enough yet myself."

After he was in bed he read the selected letters of Lucille to her sister. One was exceptionally long:

"In writing this way about Sam to you, Barb, I guess I'm sort of explaining things to myself. From your last letter I know you have been doing a lot of reading between the lines, and I guess it is time to tell you. It is funny, but I would not want to tell you all this if it had not been— excuse me, dear—for you and Roger. And you did have the guts to get out of it. It had no future and maybe this doesn't have any either, but I am living too intensely in the present to have much thought of the future. I guess it was that way with Roger for a time. Maybe everybody thinks their own infatuation is unique, and maybe in some funny way it is always alike for everyone. But how can one admit that?

"I have an awful time keeping myself from getting too elfin in this letter. I keep wanting to capitalize things and underline things and write Ha Ha here and there like some schoolgirl. I will put capitals on one thing. I am a Fallen Woman, I guess. Shameless. It is easy to say I was lonely. And I was vulnerable. But it does not to any extent explain why it should have been Sam—and continues to be Sam.

"I told you his age and his background and so on in other letters, but I didn't describe him for you. He is almost six inches over six feet tall, and he has a long sallow homely face and eyes so pale they have hardly any color at all. He has dark stringy hair. He is a great long gnarled gristly slab of a man, all knuckles and angles, but he has a curious kind of style. Something in the way he moves, the way he walks and dresses and gets in and out of chairs. He looks cruel and forceful, and no one has ever made me feel so incredibly girlish.

"He did not make any passes, Barb. He just is not that sort of man. He was kind to me, and we had fun. And I really don't think anyone . . . that is to say either one of us, thought it would become anything else. But he was so terribly depressed about a tax thing, and he called me up long distance and he sounded weary and depressed and sick at heart and he asked me to come to him. Just like that! It was absurd. I hung up on him. What did he think I was? Where did he get all that confidence? And twelve hours later while I was packing my smallest suitcase and driving out to catch the little airplane to Jacksonville, I was still telling myself it was ridiculous. I certainly didn't owe him anything like that. How could he expect me to come on the run?

"I was absolutely terrified, believe me. He is such a powerful animal, and there is such an aura of force and cruelty, I felt as if I had been hypnotized into becoming some sort of sacrificial creature. But he was so gentle! And really not confident at all. And we were funny and shy. Like honeymoon kids somehow, which was the last thing I expected. But now I can hardly remember what it was like then, dear. Because it has become so much. If I had any lingering doubts about leaving Kelsey, they are gone now. I do not want to be vulgar in this letter, but Kelsey made love as if he were trying to get a berth on the Olympic team. I was an obedient bit of athletic equipment, alert to all the clues and signals, and he often gave me the feeling that if afterward I cheered and applauded he would spring up and take bows. If I failed to simulate a frantic ecstasy, he took it as an insult to his talent. But Sam concerns himself with me. I never knew it could be possible to laugh aloud just for joy when making love. I'd always been sort of anxious and earnest about it, and sort of dismally convinced in my heart of hearts that I was really not very sexy. But Sam has turned me into an absolute glutton. I have to keep proving the same miracle to myself, over and over. I'm such a shameless yearning wench that all he has to do is look at me just so and I turn humid and my knees start to sag no matter where I am. So I guess I never really knew who I was. I am not sure I am what Sam has made me, either. Perhaps it is a swing of the pendulum. But while it continues it is at least a very precious sickness. I want nothing beyond his great long knotty frame stretched out beside me, his slow hands and his love words. I was never all the way alive until now. When you told me about Roger I only pretended to understand. I thought I did, but in a little cold part of my Puritan soul I was aghast at my kid sister being so compulsive about sensuality, and perhaps I thought you were of some coarser fabric than I. But now, bless you, I know what you were trying to tell me, and I now respect what strength it must have taken for you to end it with such a terrible abruptness. If I were to suddenly be told I could never touch Sam again, I would rend my hair, roll in ashes and sit on public streets howling like a dog. So now you know the best or the worst of me, Barb. But we can perhaps understand each other more than ever before. The only flaw in all this electric happiness is the awareness of sin. We try to keep it quiet, but I do not think anyone can look at me without knowing. He has a little house in the woods. He calls it a shack, but it is really solid and cozy. I am at the shack now, writing this, waiting for the sound of his car on the little private dirt road, knowing my heart will jump up into my throat when I hear it. Here I am in an odd garment, one of his white shirts, the sleeves rolled up, the shoulder seams down almost to my elbows, comfortably aware he will find it a highly sexy costume. I have just enough perfume, and my bare toes are pink and lonely, and little shudders of come-what-may run up and down my ribs. You see, dear, I have fallen into the habit of telling you more than I could tell you face to face. But there is no one else to talk to this way."

After he had read the other letters and had turned out the light, he kept thinking back to this letter. He wondered about Roger. And he found himself wishing, with unexpected force, that he had known Lucille Larrimore Hanson. She had been so unusually articulate in her letters, he knew he would have liked her if he could have met her. It seemed wasteful and unfair.

A dream of Lucille awoke him in the night. It was vivid, and close to nightmare. He was sweaty when he awoke. She had been in a huge glass jar, like a laboratory specimen, naked, adrift in clear fluid, her blonde hair floating wide. She kept turning, bumping the sides in a slow movement as though there was a current within the jar. Then Janey spoke to him abruptly over some sort of public address system, her voice metallic. "You were too late, Paul. You are always too early or too late. But you never listen. It never happens right. It is never going to."

He went up the stairs to find Janey and get her away from the microphone before everyone heard what she was saying to him. But he got into the wrong room where Rufus Nile, prancing and puffing, was working upon a figure on a slab. The figure was Barbara. Water poured from her mouth and nose. Nile was cutting her clothing off with little gold scissors. He beamed at Stanial. "Get the other jar ready, boy. She wanted you to help."

He broke out of the sleep filled with inexplicable guilt. He sat on the edge of the bed in the darkness of the room and smoked a cigarette. The air-conditioner masked the sounds of the night. It made him feel as if the room were in transit, on some strange vehicle moving steadily through the night.

# Five

AUGUSTUS DUMAS GABLE, in his Jacksonville hotel room, wiped his face on a hand towel and hoped there was nothing wrong with his heart, no small flaw as yet undetected, because it would be a tragic irony to lose it all that way after finally getting so close to making it. He did not know how much more of it he could endure. One moment he would feel cold and chilled and hollow, convinced of failure, depressed beyond words. Without warning a great hot shuddering flood of triumph would well through him and he would want to yell, stand on his head and giggle.

The unexpected delay in the decision was the worst part of it. Maybe something was going wrong, but he did not dare ask. These tax boys had to be dealt with delicately. You could dicker with them on a rational basis. Once a citizen had bitched his returns just enough to give them an opening, their objective was to grab all the golden eggs possible without destroying the goose. That meant a settlement just short of the point where the citizen would say the hell with it and take his chances in court. But if you tried to hustle them or con them or, God forbid, try a little discreet bribery, they would smile sadly, slay the goose and pluck him clean. He knew he had gone just as far as he dared, and the rest of it was the waiting.

Long ago Gus Gable had been deeply amused when he had heard Willie Sutton's answer to the question as to why he had robbed banks. Because that's where the money is. Gus was sufficiently objective to realize his own motives had been identical. He had guessed where the money would be, and prepared himself for participation. He had supported himself as a bookkeeper while he had gone after the law degree. After his third, and at last successful attempt to get admitted to the bar, he had stayed with the bookkeeping rather than the practice of law, and gone after the CPA. He passed that with less trouble. And then he began to prove he had been right. A tax attorney who is also a CPA is a rare and valued animal. As he began to thrive, he continued to live small and put the additional income into employees who could take the dog-work off his shoulders. Now he had busy offices on the second floor of Sam Kimber's building, and he represented half the business interests in the county. Find an obscure but totally legitimate precedent whereby a man can save an unexpected $500 on an annual tax bill, and at his next club meeting he will sing the praises of Gus Gable. And better yet, the word gets around, "When you're in trouble, get hold of Gus."

It was a legitimate recommendation. He had kept his contacts with the tax people on a fruitful level of mutual co-operation. He had not lied or fudged the figures for any client. In another time, in another place, Gus Gable might have been a guide in rough country, and with the same incomparable thoroughness he would have known every obscure track, every water hole, every sign of game and weather.

With great care and hope and patience he had been tucking money aside and awaiting a chance. He was not married. He had no dependents. He had no expensive personal habits. He had seen lesser men take wild gambles and hit unexpected jackpots. He knew he did not have the stomach for the gambles. He had to find absolutely the correct, the flawless circumstances, and he had sorted out and discarded, reluctantly, several promising situations in the past three years. And now he knew it was within his grasp, courtesy of Sam Kimber.

In one sense it would be a violation of an ethical relationship. When Sam learned the whole story, as was unavoidable, he might be furious, but given time to think it over he would see the reasons. Gus was merely picking up the slack that would go to someone else otherwise, and at the same time helping Sam out of a hole with more alacrity than might have happened otherwise.

In its simplest sense, Sam's tax problem meant he was going to have to unload asset values. And Gus Gable was going to be right there to pick them up. With a little help.

And when it was over, Gus Gable was going to have a fat piece of money tucked away, and life was going to change. He was forty-two years old, and he knew he had waited long enough. It would be legal money, his beyond the shadow of a doubt. He found it difficult to think beyond the actual fact of the money. The images beyond the money were vague. They were like the color plates in magazine advertisements. Gus Gable, at the flying bridge of his custom Rybovitch, bringing a record tuna back to the dock at Cat Cay. Gus

Gable at the wheel of his white XK-Jag. Gus Gable in Rome. And, undefined but inevitable, was the Golden Girl—beside him on the flying bridge, beside him in the car, beside him at the sidewalk cafe—merry and laughing and dear. Six months of work alternating with six months of play for the rest of his life.

He found it mildly incongruous at times, a dream that could not happen. He was forty-two, and his dark hair was thin, and his belly was soft, and his brown eyes were weak behind the astigmatic lenses. He had an office pallor, a J. C. Penney wardrobe, a voice husked by twenty cheap cigars a day, a stomach made delicate by too many years of fried foods, a shabby furnished apartment with indifferent maid service, a three-year-old Chevy which he drove badly, and no hobbies at all. For the past few years he had been grossing about seventy thousand, putting forty back into salaries and overhead, and, after taxes and living expenses, investing between fifteen and eighteen thousand a year in blue chip securities. On an average of once a month he would drive over to Tampa on a Saturday, register at a place where he was known as Robert Warren, phone the right number and be sent a blonde whore on an overnight basis, receiving always a clean, reasonably attractive and competent one, a service to be expected by a steady customer who paid well, caused no trouble and did not demand anything out of the ordinary. Sometimes he would get the same one several times running, but he never requested one by name. They were not the Golden Girl. They were just mild, rather dull-minded women who talked aimlessly about their daytime jobs, their kids in school, the men who ran out on them. In the beginning, when he had first started to use the number, they had sent some who were too young or too skinny or who drank too much, and one who was a hysterical amateur, but he had complained each time and so, for the past four years none had been really unsuitable. He would keep them until mid-morning on Sunday, and then nap until late afternoon when he checked out and drove back home.

But the money was going to change it all, somehow. Change pallor to bronze, flatten the belly, improve his reflexes, enable him to find the Golden Girl and, having found her, make her love him for his own sake, with the money just an incidental thing they could both enjoy. And he would know how to talk to her and make her laugh. And everybody would see her with him and envy him.

He wiped his face again and cleaned his glasses. He opened his brief case and took out the summary sheets on a pending hearing, but the figures and ratios made no sense to him. As he was putting them away the phone rang, and he lunged across the bed and caught it before the second ring.

"Gus?"

"Right here, Clarence. Ready and waiting."

"It just came downstairs. To round it off, two hundred and thirty-one thousand three hundred. Sixty days' grace. The formal notification goes out Monday. Make you happy?"

"Clarence, old friend, I will say gratified. It will squeeze Sam badly, but I think it is eminently fair all around. His acceptance will be automatic. And I am indebted to you."

"Sorry about the additional delay but it was one of those things. Compromise settlements have gotten some nasty publicity, so some additional review was in order. We wouldn't want Kimber crowing about how light he got off, you know."

"It's hardly light. You have my word, Clarence, and you've had the total picture in hand. He couldn't stand more."

"Do I have to tell you you don't know a thing until formal notification?"

"I will spread it around immediately, old friend, so that your whole shop will never trust me again."

"I had to mention it."

"Of course, dear boy."

As soon as that call was over, Gus Gable placed a long-distance call to Charlie Diller at the Citrus Central Bank and Trust Company, to the private number that did not go through the bank switchboard. To Gus's annoyance, Diller's girl answered. He slurred and deepened his tone and said he was a Mr. Warren calling from Jacksonville, knowing that city would be key word enough for Charlie. The girl said he had stepped out of his office for just a moment, and could he hold on, please. Moments later Charlie said, "Hello? I . . . I've been waiting to hear from you."

"It's approved on a sixty-day basis, so you can start clearing the rails."

"Well . . . I suppose it's okay to go ahead."

"I can safely say this is no time for you to even sound as if you're dragging your feet, Charlie. You have the blank notes I signed and you have the certificates and you have a personal piece of the pie, and so I truly suggest you jam it through your loan committee with all the muscle you've got, and I want it sitting in that special account today."

"Now see here!"

"Charlie, the special teasing and pleading is over and the deal was made, and so maybe I don't sound entirely respectful, but the private letter of agreement with your name on it is in my file just like the other copy is in yours, and if I hesitate a little you should jack me up the same way I'm doing it to you now."

"But I keep wondering why you're so certain he'll take this way out."

"Because it's his best move, and I can prove to him it's his best move, and Mister Sam has never done the second best thing in his life."

"I'll get on it right away," Charlie said with a little more enthusiasm.

"And my next call is to him."

Gus placed a person-to-person call to Sam Kimber. He heard Angie Powell telling the operator Mr. Kimber was out and they did not know when he would return, and so he asked to speak to Angie.

"Well hi, Gus," she said. "Honest, it isn't a gag. We just plain don't know where he is. I tried the shack awhile back but there wasn't any answer out there. You know, he almost always lets us know, but he isn't himself, not since that Lucille drowned. He's like in a daze or something, like he doesn't give a darn. Honest, I put all these letters on his desk and he was in here for an hour early, but when he left I came in and he didn't even sign them. I don't think he even looked at them. I don't know what he was doing in here all that time. We closed up yesterday to go to the funeral and I heard that after everybody left he was still there, just sitting in his car. Is there anything I can do?"

"I guess the best thing to do is take a confidential message for him, Angie, and try to get it to him as soon as you can locate him. Tell him it went through. Tell him it is six thousand three hundred and something over my last estimate, with sixty days to pay it off."

"Six thousand three over. Gee, Gus, I know that a week ago this would have had him feeling relieved, but now I've got the feeling I could tell him and he'd just give me a blank look."

"I'll start back right away, tell him, and we'll go over it together and figure the best way to do it. And would you phone downstairs and tell Betty I should be in my office by three o'clock at the latest, and I want Jimmy and Roscoe in my office by three-thirty with the Juice-Master audit. And you set me up with Mister Sam for five o'clock if you can, Angie honey."

"All I can do is try, Gus."

When Angie Powell came out of Sam Kimber's private office, Paul Stanial looked up from his magazine with one heavy black eyebrow raised in inquiry. She read the expression and said, "Not him, sir. Somebody else trying to get in touch with him." She went to her desk and Paul listened as she placed a call to somebody named Betty and relayed instructions from somebody named Gus. The older woman in the ante-office had gone downstairs with an armful of file folders, and for the first time Paul Stanial was alone with the most girl he had seen in a long time. After she had proven she was at least an inch taller than his five foot eleven, it had shocked him to see she was wearing sandals with no suggestion of a heel lift. It awed him to wonder what she would be like in four-inch heels with her hair teased into one of those towering beehives.

He decided that Sam Kimber, at six and a half feet, kept her around as an office playmate built to scale. But during the long time of waiting he had learned that she was more than an ornament. Working at top speed and with apparently flawless efficiency, she handled calls and visitors and small decisions with a bright confidence. Her dark gold hair was in lively curls which bounced when she walked. She wore a lemon-yellow skirt and an off-white blouse. She was structured supremely to scale, even to having a little more face, more gleaming teeth and larger eyes than lesser creatures. He estimated her at a minimum hundred and sixty pounds, and when first watching her thought her snugly girdled, then changed his mind and decided the lack of bounce and shake was due merely to a good taut musculature, an athletic solidity. Early twenties, he guessed. No rings on her fingers. No jewelry at all. A scent of soap and flower perfume. In spite of the sturdy profusion of breast and hip and sculptured calf, and the confident efficiency with which she worked, she gave an elusive and odd impression of childishness. He thought it might be because of her voice, pitched rather high, and with the clarity of a child's voice, combined with a sort of solemn expression of blankness when her face was in repose.

She yanked a document out of her electric typewriter, sorted the copies and took one copy over and put it on the desk of the older woman. The office setup had surprised Paul Stanial. Aside from the impressive modern decor and the obvious employee discipline and good spirits, he noted a high degree of office automation.

"I guess Mr. Kimber has a lot of varied business interests," he said.

"We sure have a lot of letterheads to keep straight," she said, smiling. "The groves and the land management and the contracting and all. But this is sort of a slack time. A good time to catch up on things. The housing jobs tapered off, and there aren't any bid contracts going on right now. I sure like it better when it's a madhouse around here. I'm a horse for work."

"Is Mr. Kimber taking it easier these days?"

He knew from her immediate change of expression he had gone a little too far. "Like I told you an hour ago, Mr. Stanial, I'm Mister Sam's private and confidential secretary, and if you could tell me what it is you've got on your mind, I might save you a lot of waiting around. I know from the master index we've never had one thing to do with North Atlantic Mutual, and if you have any idea of selling him anything, you won't get past word three."

"I'm not selling anything, Miss Powell. This is just a routine insurance investigation."

She went back and sat on the corner of her desk, folded strong brown arms and frowned at him. "But if it's a routine thing, maybe you wouldn't have to worry him with it."

"The investigation is routine, but the particular . . . involvement . . . his relationship to it, is a personal matter and I think he'd rather I kept it on a personal basis."

Her eyes widened momentarily and she pursed her lips. "Now it just wouldn't happen to be insurance on that Mrs. Hanson, would it?"

Stanial faked clumsy surprise and said, "It's a personal matter."

"He won't take kindly to you bothering him about her."

"If anybody refuses to cooperate, all I can do is make a negative report."

"So it is about her!"

"I didn't say it was."

"I guess he's the one you have to talk to. I don't know anything about that woman. And didn't want to know." A harshness had crept into her tone. She sat at her desk and rolled fresh paper into the typewriter. Stanial decided the big husky girl probably had emotional cause for complaint.

"Have you worked for Mr. Kimber long?"

"Three years," she said abruptly.

Carefully casual, he said, "I guess it's only natural you'd feel some resentment toward Lucille Hanson."

For a few moments her hands rested on the keys. She turned and looked at him. It was not the expression he expected. It was a puzzled look. "Why should I resent her? I wouldn't resent any of Mister Sam's women unless they tried to hurt him some way, and if they did, I figure he can take care of himself. It's man's way to want women, and I don't have to understand it, do I? I can feel sorrow and pity it should be so, but it is the burden man brought out of the Garden, and he sins and whether or not he is forgiven is up to God. And I don't have to understand why there's women who entice men and make them drunk on the dirty habits of the flesh, without even the words of the church to make it halfway clean in God's eyes. But I don't have to know anything about those women, or have any wonderment about them, Mr. Stanial. I'm sorry she died in the middle of her dirty ways before he got sick of her, so now he confuses mourning with his unsatisfied lust. But he'll get over it, and there'll be another one, and another one after that, and when the fires of the body begin to die, I pray he'll make his peace with God and cleanse himself." Her voice had taken on a singsong quality, faintly reminiscent of a revival sermon. She gave a small shiver and smiled at him and said in a normal tone, "There's no cause I should resent that woman."

"I'm sorry. I didn't understand."

"Most people don't understand. It doesn't bother me. Evil doesn't touch me, Mr. Stanial. It's my fate men should come snuffling around me with all their winks and sly ways, staring at me and trying to brush their hands against me. God made me desirable to men so as to keep testing me. I am His lamb. When I was fifteen I spent two days and two nights on my knees asking Him if I should hide my body from the world of men and spend my life in prayer. But He told me to live in the world and spurn the tempters and the deceivers because from my example some of them might find the Kingdom of Heaven. My body is the temple of the Lord, and I keep it clean and strong and unsoiled." Again she made the abrupt change from singsong to normal conversation. "I don't expect many people to understand, Mr. Stanial."

"Does Mr. Kimber?"

She sighed. "Sort of, I guess. The only thing he won't allow is me preaching at him. He says we all have to go our own way and find out things in our own time. But, golly, it sure is taking him a long time to see the error of his ways. Sometimes I feel right discouraged about Mister Sam. And I get blue. But if I go out and run a few miles or swim a few miles and get myself tuckered, I feel better. You look like you have a strong healthy body, Mr. Stanial, but you've smoked two cigarettes since you sat down there, and it's a shame you have to do that to yourself." She frowned and shook her head. "I surely wish I knew where that man went off to. He might not even come in at all. I can't promise you a thing."

Paul stood up. "Suppose I phone back in and find out if you've heard anything."

"I'll be having Mrs. Nimmits bring some lunch in for me, so I'll be right here all day. You want I should tell him what you want to see him about if he comes in?"

He smiled at her. "You will anyway, won't you?"

"Sure, but I wondered if you'd ask me not to."

"You do what you think is best, Miss Powell."


It was quarter to eleven when Stanial turned into the shell drive at the Hanson estate on Lake Larra. The main house, completely screened from the road by the heavy tropical plantings, was an imposing but informal frame structure of weathered cypress trimmed with white, with a low modern wing in conflict with the roof lines of the older part. He parked and got out and looked toward the lake and saw the boat house through the trees. He found the mouth of the winding path, white shell under the shadows and the hanging beards of Spanish moss. The lake glinted blue beyond the boat house. He saw Hanson's car parked off to the side, and saw the outside staircase leading up to the living quarters.

As Stanial climbed the stairs to the upper level, Kelsey Hanson, in shiny dark-blue swim trunks, appeared on the open landing and said, "Hold it right there. What do you want?"

Stanial stopped and looked up at him. Hanson was an impressive brute, sun-browned, heavily muscled, his hair and brows and lashes bleached almost white by the sun. He had an ugly, unfriendly expression on his face. Though the features were fleshy, it was a reasonably handsome face. He looked like the lifeguard getting ready to throw the ninety-eight-pound weakling off the beach. At his second appraisal, Stanial saw that the heavy tan disguised considerable physical deterioration. The waist was soft and had thickened. The fibrous muscles bulged under a recent layer of fat. The face untanned would have looked puffy and bloated.

"I want to talk to you about your wife's insurance."

"What about it?"

"There are some questions that I . . ."

"Put them in a letter, pal."

"It will only take a few minutes of your . . ."

"You've used it all up already, pal. So turn around and paddle right back down the stairs."

Stanial, grinning inwardly at the old doctor's advice, glared up at Hanson and headed directly toward him, saying loudly and angrily, "You silly bastard, I'm investigating your wife's suicide, and I'm not a door-to-door salesman, and I'm cleared with the police, and if you keep up this line of crap, I'll give you problems you never heard of before." As he took the last step up onto the landing, Hanson backed away from him.

"Why didn't you say so, pal?"

"I just did."

"You've got no idea the pests coming around here, trying to . . . Listen, Lucille didn't kill herself."

"That's what we're trying to ascertain, one way or the other, and if you can spare a little of your invaluable time, Mr. Hanson . . ."

"Hell, I've got nothing but time, fella." Hanson's smile was imploringly charming and self-deprecatory. "Come on in and set where it's cool. I didn't mean to get off on the wrong foot. No hard feelings. I've been under a terrible strain lately."

Stanial had seen this disease before. Emptiness. Hanson seemed incapable of projecting any unqualified emotion. Anger, amusement, love, hate, jealousy—they would all be hollowed out and turned into masks by the basic uncertainty in the man's eyes, his flavor of apology.

"No hard feelings, of course," Stanial said and shook hands. He went inside with Hanson and refused the offer of coffee or a drink. It was a long studio room with dark rough paneling, heavy masculine furniture, built-in music system, coquina rock fireplace and a sizeable bar.

"Now what is this crap about Lucille?" Hanson demanded. "Who came up with a weird idea like that?"

"All we can say so far is that it's a possibility. I understand you and she were legally separated."

"For almost a year now."

"Would you say it was her fault the marriage broke up?"

"Now wait a minute. I'm not convinced it was broken up for good."

"You think she was going to come to her senses?"

"Well, I certainly hoped so. And I was willing to take her back the minute she said the word. As to it being her fault, I guess we were both at fault. I got a little out of line, I guess. And got caught. And she made too much of a big thing of it. Hell, it wasn't as if I'd gotten serious about somebody else. It was just . . . you know . . . one of those things. They aren't important unless you want to make them important. And Lu never seemed to really fit in down here. At first I thought she would. And I guess she did too. Anyway, we were taking a one-year break, and I've got no proof she wouldn't have come back to me."

"You were going to try to get her back?"

"Certainly!"

"In spite of the fact she'd become intimate with Samuel Kimber?"

Hanson flinched as though he'd been struck. "You've been prying around, Mr. . . ." He looked at the card Paul had given him. "Mr. Stanial. You've got no proof of that."

"It's a reasonable certainty, Mr. Hanson."

"I . . . I guess so. But it's the kind of thing you don't want to think about. I just can't understand it. Lucille was such a . . . careful person. Fastidious. You know? And a good education. And that guy Kimber is twice her age, and he's a great big crude son of a bitch. How he ever got her into the sack I'll never know. That was the last time I saw her to talk to. Five or six months ago, after people had started to gossip about them. I had to find out if it was so. But she wouldn't even answer any questions. She was polite and she smiled at me, and she said we'd made a bargain that she would wait one year before asking for a divorce, and when the year was up she would tell me what she had decided to do. I told her I'd heard she was running around with Sam Kimber. She said you hear all kinds of things if you listen long enough, and then she got into her car and drove away. That was the last time I ever saw her."

"But you'd have taken her back, even if it was true?"

"What the hell is that to you?"

"Just investigating possibilities, Mr. Hanson. What if she wanted to come back and thought that by her relationship with Kimber she'd spoiled her chances. And then, out of guilt and remorse, she killed herself."

"Oh no. She *knew* I'd take her back."

"Because she knew that if you didn't, your father was going to throw you out?"

Hanson looked startled. "Who the hell *have* you been talking to, friend? That might be the story going around, but it isn't true. Sure, old John threatened that, but he's been threatening it ever since I was seventeen years old, and the old lady has never let him do it. Why should he follow through this time? I'd take her back because . . . I wanted her back."

"Would you say she was emotionally unstable?"

"Lucille? Well, about a few things I guess. She always took everything too seriously. Not many laughs. I don't know if that means anything."

"So she probably took Mr. Kimber seriously."

"I . . . Yes, I guess she would."

"And then if he decided to end the affair?"

Hanson looked at him with an almost anguished irritation. "I don't know what the *hell* you're trying to do. I didn't know she *had* any insurance. Who gets it, anyway?"

"Her mother and her sister equally."

"Honest to God, Mr. Stanial, I can't see Lu killing herself, or doing it that way. She was as strong a swimmer as I am. Drowning yourself isn't easy when you're at home in the water. All your instincts are against it."

"Then isn't it more logical than an accidental drowning?"

"That's hard to take too, but that's what everybody says. It would make more sense to say somebody drowned her. But not too much more sense. Middle of the day. That isn't as big a lake as this one. How could you know somebody didn't have a pair of binoculars on you? From where she drowned, you can see the houses across the way. And how in the world would anybody do it without leaving a mark on her? Lu didn't look husky, but she was a strong woman. Maybe she had too much heat and passed out in the water. Or had food poisoning and fainted. Everybody who wanted to give me the needle would tell me how damn sassy she looked lately. Maybe she was taking pills for something and took too many. How the hell are you ever going to find out?"

"If we can establish a reasonable assumption of suicide, we'll fight paying off on the double indemnity provision."

Hanson grimaced. "That makes it a lot clearer, pal. Why should I help you save your cruddy money?"

"The company's money, not mine."

"If she left a note, it would save you a lot of trouble."

"Maybe she did."

"What does that mean?"

"Kimber has a lot of local influence, and he wouldn't want to be mentioned in anything like that, would he?"

"What are you smoking lately?"

"If she mailed you a note, it might make you look bad, Hanson."

Hanson looked genuinely startled and then he laughed, but it was not a mirthful sound. "Could I look much worse no matter how the cards fall? And Kimber isn't that big, and never will be." And then, abruptly, Hanson changed personalities. It had been a long time since Stanial had been caught off guard. Yet he began to see why the kind of woman who had written those letters could have seen something of value and substance in Kelsey Hanson. "I've lost things here and there, Stanial. Chances, mostly. And when they're gone, it's the easiest thing in the world to tell yourself you didn't want them anyway. But I wasn't thinking of Lu as a chance. Old John was, I guess. I didn't know she was a chance until she was gone and I knew I'd blown it. So I tried to tell myself I didn't want her anyway. Sometimes, I guess, the old rationalizations stop working. But I wanted another crack at the chance Lu represented. I wanted it so bad I ached. Not on account of the old man's threat. For me, this time. I don't like myself very much, Stanial. I thought I might see if I could find out why, and maybe it would be a starting point . . . to something or other. I started out with great dedication, taking courses, trying to find some meaning to me and some meaning to life. And when I had some half-answers, I was going to go to Lu and tell her. But those cerebral types didn't have the answers, and the answers weren't in their books. I tried a psychiatrist, and after four sessions he told me my problem was emotional immaturity based on there always being somebody around to clean up the mess for me. And he said a couple of years of deep analysis might help, but no guarantee. So I sold myself another dream. I'd worked it out my own way. But I wasn't working anything out. I was using the tragic figure image on some earnest juicy little college girls, telling myself I was relegating sex to its proper perspective, and telling myself one of them would come up with a bull session idea worth checking out. But Lu died. And it killed that little part I was playing. And I don't know what the hell to do with myself now. Poor little rich boy. I got the years to use up now. Somehow." He gave Paul an odd smile. "And I'm not looking forward to one damn minute of any one of them, pal. I muffed the last chance there was."

"Unless you find yourself another."

"Where, pal?"

Stanial looked at the comfortable room and the wide windows and the blue lake. "Any place but here. Thirty are you? Five years from now you'll look fifty."

"Sorry I brought it up. I don't need you patting me on the head."

There was the nearby sound of a powerful marine engine audible over the hum of the air-conditioning, and three short blasts on a horn. Hanson got up quickly and went out and Stanial followed more slowly. A teak and mahogany runabout, beautifully maintained, floated about twenty feet from the dock below. The woman at the wheel turned the key off and smiled up. Two small children in bulky orange life vests sat on the transom seat looking solemnly up.

"Courier service, dearie. Lorna's phone is out and so is mine and probably yours is too. Festivities at Stu and Lorna's, Kelse. Like five." She was a freckled, gingery, sturdy little woman with a trim and hearty figure. She arched her back slightly and said, "Bring your silent chum too, sweetie."

"He's just here on insurance," Hanson said with no attempt at an introduction. "Tell you about it later."

"Let's go *fast*, Mom," one of the children said pleadingly.

The woman waved her hand, gunned the engine and took off in a wide sparkling curve.

"She never liked Lu," Hanson said.

"I beg your pardon?"

"Mrs. Brye. They're neighbors. She never cared much for Lu. I remember Lu saying Suey was trivial. What the hell did she expect Suey to do? Go picket the White House?" He turned and gave Stanial an absent nod. He looked at his watch. "Sorry I can't help you, pal. I've got a tennis date. Got to sweat out the old before I pour in the new."

As Stanial was going down the stairs, Hanson called after

him, "If you turn up anything, will you let me know about it?"

"If you'd like."

"I'd like. Thanks."

Stanial went directly to the motel. Barbara was not in her room. He left the car and walked toward town and found her at the counter of the first small lunchroom he came to. After her start of surprise, her smile for him was quick and warm.

After he had ordered and the counter girl moved away, he said in a low voice, "One unpleasant thing you can do, and probably pointless. Hanson has me tabbed as a cold-hearted bastard. You can enhance the image."

"Love to."

"Thanks. Stu and Lorna. Would that be the Keavers?"

"Yes."

"And if you called up to say you were lonesome, you'd get invited to cocktails and dinner. And when the gathering gets damp enough, you can start whining about me, and what I'm trying to prove. Then see if you can get Kelsey onto his thesis that even murder, absurd as it is, is more plausible than suicide. Get them all playing the game, if you can stand it."

"Paul! Do you really think any of those people . . ."

"No. But they live here. We don't. Two objectives. They may spread a little light on motive, without knowing it. Remember anything that doesn't sound too insane. Tomorrow that conversation will spread all over town. And that might open something else up. Think you can do it?" She held her hand out, palm up. "What's that for?"

"For a dime for that phone over there."

She came back looking smug. "She said she was glad I called because it proved her phone was working again. Stu will swing by and pick me up about four-thirty on his way home, and bring me back when it's over."

"If it gets out of hand, find a phone and call me at the motel and then go on out onto the road and I'll pick you up."

"I'm competent, Paul. Now I have sort of a . . . hard thing to do. Kelsey said I could take care of Lu's things, and if I came across anything I thought he might want, I could have it sent to him. I called Mrs. Carey and she said I could have the key any time. The things she had with her at that beach, they brought them from the court house and left them in the apartment. And her car is there. I talked to her lawyer about it, on the phone. Walter Ennis. He seems quite nice.

He's fixing it so I can get the money out of her checking account. There isn't much, he says. A little over eighty dollars. And I'm to find the car title and give it to him, and the car keys, and he'll sell it for me. I'm to separate the things to . . . be shipped home, and leave the rest and he'll take care of it. But I do feel strange about going there, Paul."

"I'd like to look around too, if you wouldn't mind."

"I hoped you'd want to."

"But I may have to leave you there and come back for you."

"That will be all right. Once I get started I'll be all right."

"So let's get started now."


# Six

STANIAL HAD A two-thirty appointment with the man who had turned in the alarm about the possible drowning. The man and his family lived in a small pink cinder block house about two miles from Flamingo Lake. Children were whooping and racing and cycling through the streets and small yards. Willard Maple was a gaunt, hollow-chested man in his late twenties with large fading tattoos on both lean forearms. He was spraying shrubbery when Stanial drove up. They moved into the shade of the carport to talk.

"The way it was, Mr. Stanial, I got off shift that day at twelve noon, and it was a hot one, and when I get home Peg says lets go on over to Flamingo Lake, and I says sure. But with the futzing around and having lunch first and her calling up her sister to find out we should pick them up too, we got there maybe twenty minutes to two, Pete and Em and their one kid, and the two of us and our three, all piled into that old station wagon of mine there. There's three little roads to the lake and the way we do, if the first place is crowded we go along to the next one, and so on. But there was just the one car there, and so we agreed it was okay and I put the car in as much shade as I could find and we all come piling out and down to the beach with the gear. There was a stripedy towel spread, and a radio playing and a beach bag and woman's sandals and nobody there. It wasn't creepy right away. You don't think much about it. The four kids didn't mess up the beach because they all of them went racing off to look in the hollow stump where they'd hid some kind of treasure last time. Pete is sure it's a couple and they gone back off in the bushes. But it was my Peg pointed out the foot marks, woman-size feet going on down to the water across that maybe ten foot of clean sand all dimpled from the hard rain. Then it did seem kind of spooky. We stared way out all around and not a head nowhere. We yelled separate and all the same time and listened and didn't hear a thing. That's when we shut the kids up so good they started crying, soft like. And by then we were talking soft. Pete said we'd look like pure damn fools we report a drownding and it turns out somebody came by in a boat and took her for a ride. But Em said she wouldn't go off and leave her little battery radio running, would she? And that seemed to settle it. So Peg and me stayed and Pete went off in the wagon with Em and the kids and stopped at the Amoco station and phoned in it looked like some Mrs. Hanson had drownded and he told where. We knew the name from looking at a wallet sort of thing in the beach bag. So like we arranged, Pete left Em and the kids off to his house and came on back and made it fast enough to get here just ahead of the rescue people and the ambulance, but by then some of the gas station guys had come over and they'd told other people and we were getting a crowd, and this may sound like a terrible thing to say, but after getting the whole thing rolling like that, the thing I was most scared of was that damn fool woman coming walking along the shore and wanting to know what the hell was going on. Well, as they were getting set to get into action, there was a boat out there and a kid in a mask and flippers and the first thing you know that kid is yelling and everybody looked at him and he came a-sidestroking in towing something. They went down to meet him, and that was one husky kid, but as soon as he could stand up and take a good look at what he'd towed in, he ran a little ways and threw up. They put that oxygen thing on her for a little while, but from forty feet away you could tell it wouldn't do a damn thing for that woman. They covered her and put her into the ambulance, and by then the little road was clogged up so good they played hell sireening their way out of there. The deputy said me and Pete should make a statement, on account of we reported it, so we left Peg off with her sister and the kids and went on to town to the Sheriff's office and answered questions and signed what they wrote up. We haven't none of us been back to that same place swimming and I don't know as we ever will. A thing like that sure makes the damn water look different to you. When I think on it I can hear that little radio playing away, and her already dead under the water. I've told this enough times I don't guess I left out a thing."

"You saw the bare footprints yourself?"

"We all did, and looked at them close."

"Did she run into the water?"

"No. I wouldn't say so. She just set her stuff down and walked direct in, not fast and not slow I'd say. Steady walking, just five prints and the last one right at the edge so the toes were washed out some."

"Is that the most popular of the three roads down to the shore?"

"On account of more parking room and room to turn around easy. If there was, say, four cars there we might go along to the next one, but three or less and there's room enough. And it's better sand there. Guys trailer their boats in and launch them there sometimes."

"You didn't notice anybody turning out of that road as you were approaching it?"

"It's a straight stretch along there and I would have noticed anybody coming out of any one of those three little roads, because when you're wondering how crowded it is you notice things like that."

"Here is a rough sketch of the little beach, Mr. Maple. Would you please draw in where the towel was, the radio and the beach bag and her car?"

"You fellas really go into things thorough. The car was here, nosed up to a tree that's right here, sort of on the left part of the beach. The towel was spread out neat and flat right here. And the beach bag here on some grass at the edge of the sand, and the radio leaning against it, with the radio and the beach bag in the shade of this here same tree. The sandals were right here beside the towel, one standing up and the other across it upside down, like she kicked them off careless."

"Thanks, Mr. Maple. You're very observant. This is a lot of help."

"No help to her," Willard Maple said. "As Peg says, if she'd decided earlier and fixed a lunch, we could have been there before twelve-thirty, and I can swim good enough to haul somebody out if they weren't too far from shore, and she wasn't far out at all. Forty to fifty feet at the most. But all the ifs you can string together won't change anything already over and done."

When Stanial called Kimber's office the third time, Miss Powell said he could stop by at six o'clock, and he might have to wait but it shouldn't be a long wait. Stanial got back to Lucille's apartment at exactly three-thirty. Barbara was being resolutely casual, but Paul could sense the strain she was under. She was at the kitchen table with a metal lock box and a jewelry case.

"There's more sorting to do than I thought. I'll have to finish it up tomorrow, I guess. This was in the closet and there was a key in the jewelry case that fit it. Here's the car title for Mr. Ennis. And her personal papers. What's this, though? Is this the investment thing Mr. Kimber found for her?"

He looked it over. "It's her copy of a partnership agreement. And this shows she has a one-twelfth undivided interest in a warehouse lease held in the name of the partnership."

"She was getting ninety dollars a month. What happens to that?"

He located the appropriate clause in the partnership agreement. "The other partners buy it back for what she put in it. Seven thousand."

"And who gets that?"

"You didn't find a will, did you?"

"No."

"Then I guess Hanson is the one who gets it."

"Golly, that doesn't seem fair!"

"Maybe he won't want it. You should turn these documents over to Ennis, too. He'll want to get some kind of a release from Hanson, I'd think."

She pushed a wedding ring and an engagement ring across the table toward him. "And these. I think the diamond is good."

He picked it up, remembering the elements of a two-hour police seminar in gems. One carat, he estimated. A deep cut, a pure white.

"Very good, probably."

"Should I give it back to him?"

"Why ask me, Barbara?"

"I *hate* this sort of thing. Greed, I guess. So I want to make sentimental gestures. But, damn it all, there's really very little stuff here worth anything. When she left him, she left behind the things he'd bought her. And the wedding presents that came from his friends. She was like that. She still hadn't decided whether she was going to ask for alimony. She had so much pride. Maybe that's my problem, too. Too much pride. I want to send him his stinking diamond back, but what if I could get a thousand dollars for it? The medical bills on my mother have been sickening. And they can get worse."

"So keep it."

Her smile was wan. "That was the nudge I needed. Thanks. The wedding ring can go back to him. It's initialed inside. And those look like good little stones, too. The compromise gesture. My life is full of them. And here's a batch of photographs I guess he should have. And, for his trophy case, the marriage certificate. I might as well take this stuff with me tonight and get it over with. She rented this place furnished. There won't be much to ship back home. A couple of good pieces of luggage, some silver, some of the clothing."

"When you get it ready, I'll take care of shipping it."

"Thanks, but I'll just take it back with me and pay the overweight if there is any. I guess I'll have to tell that Mrs. Carey I'll be back tomorrow. And she'll make a big production about letting me in again."

"Didn't she give you a key?"

"There's only one."

"Where's the one your sister had?"

"I couldn't find any."

He frowned for a moment and then went and looked at the front door to the apartment. It was of the type that has to be locked with a key upon leaving.

"What's the matter, Paul?"

"I don't know. She would have taken the key to the lake."

"It isn't on her car keys and it wasn't in the beach bag or her purse."

He picked up the phone. It was dead.

"When you think of it," Barbara said, "it is sort of strange."

"I guess Sheriff Walmo must have kept it. But I'd like to ask him."


After he had left Barbara off at the motel to change for the party at the Keavers, he phoned Walmo.

"Is this line private, Sheriff?"

"Go right ahead, Mr. Stanial."

"As part of your procedure, Sheriff, did you make an inventory of the Hanson woman's belongings you gathered up at the lake?"

"Well, not real detailed. I mean not down to the lipstick in the purse and all that. But the money went on there. Six dollars and some change. And the little radio and such."

"Was there a house key?"

"Come to think of it, no, there wasn't. I did look for one."

"Didn't you think there should have been?"

"Lots of people don't lock a door around here all year round."

"I checked with Mrs. Carey. Lucille always locked the place up when she left. You have to lock it with the key. There's no snap lock. Can you remember if she left her car keys in her car at the lake?"

"Hold on just a minute." When Walmo came back on the line he said, "That's where they were. Two car keys and two other keys on a split ring. But neither of the other two keys fit her apartment door. I just don't know what they fit."

"Probably one of them fits Doctor Nile's office. Mrs. Carey is quite certain Lucille kept her house key on that ring. She was with Lucille a couple of times when she unlocked her door."

After a long silence Stanial heard Walmo's long exhalation. "I wouldn't want you should try to make something out of damn near nothing, Stanial."

"I don't want to. But I would like to know where that key went. As you can see, Sheriff, it enlarges the area of possible motive."

"*If* she had something worth taking. I can tell you somebody hasn't got that key. Sam Kimber. Day after she died he talked me into giving him a note to Miz Cary to let him in there to pick up some private papers he said she'd been working on. Far as I know he did just that. He picked them up."

"Or said he did?"

"Business slow out of your office this time of year?"

"What do you mean?"

"If you have to have every little thing explained, you could keep this going a long time. Maybe there's some good explanation about that key. You sure you know the rules of evidence?"

"Sheriff, I didn't make this contact to tell you I had anything worth re-opening your investigation. I just called to ask a question. When I do have anything, I will certainly let you know."

"You do that."

After Stanial hung up, he stretched out on his motel bed and examined the fragility of the structure of supposition he was erecting. X was the unknown quantity, the drowner. He was asking quite a bit of X. He had to be in a position to know that Lucille had something of value in her apartment. He had to follow her to the lake, or make a date to meet her there. He had to drown her without leaving a mark on her or on the sand, then know which of three keys that were not car keys to take off the key ring, having previously figured out how to get in and out of the apartment without being seen. But to take something from the apartment, was it necessary to drown the woman beforehand? Only if, after it was taken, she was the only one who would know who took it.

Or, there could have been no planning at all, murder on impulse and the rest of it improvised, benefiting from luck.

A key that disappeared was stolen, borrowed or lost. Or taken from her effects afterward. Or Kimber's request to enter the apartment could have been a false trail, a monstrous deviousness.

In the past he had built structures more solid than this one and had discarded them because they did not feel right. They were contrived, and could lead only to absurdity. But this *seemed* right. It made the back of his neck tingle. And that, he thought, is one remarkable investigative tool—a responsive neck.

And maybe the key had been a symbol to her of everything that had gone wrong with her life, and so she had hurled it into the brush before swimming out, floating, steeling herself to that final effort of rejection, that first, convulsive inhalation of lake water.

Most murder was made of other materials. Most murder was somebody dazed, sitting in a crowded bloody kitchen, mumbling they didn't mean to do it.

You could not get emotionally involved with that. You just did what had to be done as quickly as you could, the way you hold your breath and clean up a dog's mess.

But you could get involved here, he thought. In ways you don't need. Like being able, right now, to see with a fearful clarity the precise way Barbara's hair lies against the gentle area behind her ear, and the round and fluent padding of the socket of the hip, matching with such a curious elegance the neighbor concavity of the waist. A girl austere, complex and too remote, and any commitment would be full of the severe kinetics of demand. Better, he thought, the brown and obvious and unvowing frolickers of North Miami Beach, the twisters, the yea-sayers, the beach and bar release for the ex-cop pooped from a day investigating supermarket pilferage. This one's tokens would be real hearts and real flowers, and all he had left in stock was candy and wax.

But exactly who the hell had Roger been?

Suddenly, from his subconscious, came the certainty that he knew what the other key would fit. Kimber's shack.

And the pending interview with Kimber became just that much more crucial.

Sam Kimber was beginning to take a more specific form. He sensed that danger might lie in underestimating the man.


Gus Gable had his coat off and there was a scurf of cigar ashes down the front of his white shirt. The papers were spread out on Sam's desk. Sam was stretched out on the big red leather couch, a can of beer in his hand, his eyes half closed. His slacks and sport shirt were badly wrinkled, and he had a twenty-four hour stubble of gray beard on his long sad cheeks and lantern jaw.

Gus looked at him with exasperation. "I can truly say, Sam, you don't seem to get the significance of getting moving on this thing."

Sam said idly, "You've done a fine job and I can understand you want to see it all the way through. Fine, Gus. But we'll get the money to them. Don't you fret."

Gus walked over and looked down at him. "It isn't that. Sure. They'll get the money. They always do. It's how to raise it the best possible way. And that means starting right now. I've figured out just how it can be done, but I get the idea you're not listening."

Kimber yawned. "Guess I better settle down and listen, it being the only way I'm going to get rid of you."

Gus pulled a chair close and sat down. "You don't dare sell any of the land you hold because they got you classified as a land merchant, and anything you get would be taxed as straight income, right? And you got the land so damn cheap, if you raised a quarter million that way to pay them off, you'd be in the bag for two hundred thousand more on this year's taxes, so you'd get nowhere, or, if they closed the fiscal year on you, you'd be worse off. And if you unload a quarter million in liquid assets, then you bitch your chances of making the bond on the jobs you want to bid."

"Sounds right dismal," Sam murmured.

"So here's what we do. We take that tract along Flamingo Lake and that tract out beyond Beetle Creek and we put them into one package. Now if we try to incorporate a development outfit, Jacksonville is going to call it a device. So we look around fast, and we find where there's some development money looking for a home. We let it be known those two tracts can be had, if they let you in on it. We let the other guys set it up, then give you stock in return for the land. You'll have to take a beating on it, Sam, because you're in a pocket. You won't be able to have control. It would look funny. Then you put up the stock as collateral with Charlie Diller for a loan big enough to pay off the tax bill. And then, after enough time has passed, you can sell the stock, pay off the loan and pay capital gains on the stock sale."

"I suppose."

"Have you listened close, Sam?"

"Doesn't it mean somebody could be picking up some prime land without hardly any damn risk at all?"

"To keep from giving you control, they'd have to come up with a good chunk into the kitty for the rest of the stock, for operating expenses and working capital."

Sam opened his eyes all the way. "That can be done with notes back and forth, boy. I may have lost a little interest in things, but I haven't lost my mind. Hell, we'd be further ahead working it through a dummy setup."

"Granted!" Gus said angrily. "And they're watching you like a tree full of hawks watching a chicken. I tell you in all truth and flat out, Sam, I've got my reputation on the line too, and sincerely, if you try one cute thing I have to get out to keep myself clean, and let them know I've gotten out. You're a big valuable client, Sam, and you've paid me a lot of money, but you try anything and they'll think we figured it out together. Then what kind of a reception do I get the next time? Listen to me, Sam. Believe me! For the rest of your life you have to be as clean . . ."

"As a whistle, Gussy. As a whistle." Sam slowly levered himself up, stood up and flipped the empty beer can into the basket beside the desk. He walked through the ante-office with that long slow slouching stride which had Gable almost trotting to keep up with him.

"Go home, Angie," he said as he passed her desk.

"When I'm finished," she said tartly.

He went into his bachelor apartment with Gus at his heels. He selected fresh clothes and tossed them onto the oversized bed.

"I want your personal assurance, Sam, you're going to do the smart thing under the circumstances."

As he slowly unbuttoned his soiled shirt, Sam Kimber said, "Summertimes, you wanted to get the stink off you, you'd grab a sliver of yella soap and go down to the creek where it ran deep and black. Trouble was, the skeeters hung out there big as humming birds with a bore rod on 'em like a leather punch. Everyday skeeters didn't bother me a damn, but those grandaddies down there could punch right on through to the marrow."

"I'm just trying to . . ."

"What you'd do, you'd trade the stink for welts. If they'd got together right, they could have wedged a man up in a tree crotch and bled him to a crust." He balled the soiled shirt, slacks, shorts and socks and dropped them into a pigskin hamper. "Found me a homemaking magazine one time in a ditch where some tourist lady flang it from her fast car and it had the goddamdedest biggest whitest shiniest bathroom in it you ever heard of. Vowed I'd get me one of them and pretty soap with a sweet smell and big soft brushes with long handles and towels big as bed sheets and thick as a young girl's wrist and I'd scrub and soak me down to the last little thin layer of hide and I'd stay in there the whole summertime long." As he adjusted the heat and force of the big adjustable shower heads, he smiled vaguely at Gus Gable and said, over the steamy roar of the water, "Funny thing, you know, for a man to break his ass all his life to buy the best bathroom in Florida." He He stepped in and closed the glass door of the giant stall, and Gus Gable wandered disconsolately back out into the bedroom. He went to the kitchen and opened himself a can of beer and felt guilty about it. That damned Kimber could drink beer all day long and his belly stayed flat. Gable had the feeling that every can of beer he had ever drunk had added its inevitable gram of fat, and he would never lose it.

A few minutes after the shower had stopped, Gus went back

into the bathroom. Sam stood at the sink with a towel knotted around his waist, shaving with a straight razor. The mirror was set high, and the oversized stainless steel sink was set into a counter placed at the right height for Sam Kimber. Gus always felt irritable in Sam's apartment. He felt dwarfed and pulpy. There were tufts of black hair on Sam's long back. Ropey muscles moved under the yellowish hide. His legs were heavily furred.

"Where were you all day, Sam?"

"Out at the shack."

"They kept trying to get you out there."

"I heard the phone ringing a few times. Didn't feel like answering."

"What did you do?"

"Walked around some. Got up at first light. Took me a bass outen the pond there, but by the time I crumbed some and fried it, I was past eating. Figure to sell it, I guess."

"Not this year, Sam. You can't afford to sell any property this year."

Sam rinsed and dried the razor, put it in the case, walrused his face in cold water and said, "How are you on my giving it away?"

"Not to a private party, Sam."

"How would you feel about the scouts?"

"I can work it up and see what it would do for you."

"You do that, Gussy." Gus followed him out of the bathroom. "I'm just not about to go back out there, not any time."

Sam put on a pale blue shirt and dark gray slacks. He went to the kitchen and, without asking Gus, made two strong drinks of bourbon over ice in chunky oversized old-fashioned glasses. He handed one to Gus, gestured with his own in silent toast, took a small swallow and said, "All dressed up and no place to go." He looked at Gus and his expression was odd, a simultaneous frown and smile, expressing a strange ironic agony. "And me a man growed," he said softly.

"What, Sam?"

Gus followed him into the living room. Sam slumped on a couch and said, "Get cleared away here, and I was thinking I might go way the hell down off the coast of Chile and see if maybe I could tie into one of those granddaddy tuna they talk about. Something I never tried."

"Maybe there'd be a chance of working something out with the marine biology people at Miami to get a partial write-off. I can look into it, Sam."

Sam stared at him and shook his head. "Don't you beat all!"

"Hell, you pay me to think of things like that. And I've saved you ten times what you've paid me."

"Might go to Orlando tonight and look up a little old red-top gal I haven't seen in three years, Gussy. Figure me a partial write-off on that? Then again, it might turn out mighty like that fried bass. Just when it's ready, you don't want it."

"What I want is to know if you'll go ahead with my proposal."

"I'll think on it."

Gus hitched forward on his chair, holding his drink between his knees. "Sam, can I speak real frank?"

"Try it and see how it goes."

"I can truly say I'm not a complete damn fool."

"Not in your line of work, Gussy."

"I have to speak up now because you're taking this all so casually, the financial jam you're in. Hell, I know the quarter million is nothing compared to your net worth if we could liquidate it slowly and carefully over a long period. But it is still serious. You'll admit that?"

"Seems to be."

"I've never mentioned this directly to you before because I didn't want to get any answers. I think I know you pretty well. You keep things to yourself. Nobody ever gets to know all there is to know."

"Keep showing the hole cards and it's showdown, and there's no fun in that."

"Sam, I've talked myself into believing that personal balance sheet we worked out gives the complete and total story. Let me finish. But I'm not a damn fool. I went back a way, Sam. Quite a few years. I tried computing net worth a different way, the way the tax people do sometimes. They take income after taxes and take off the estimated living expenses, and see how much you should have piled up over so many years, then compare it to what you say you've piled up. I went just far enough to feel glad they didn't try that with you, Sam."

Sam came smoothly to his feet. "Right now you've got my whole attention, Gus. Say what you're trying to say."

"I just . . . think you've got a hole card. I don't know how much. Cash money, probably. Maybe as little as fifty thousand or as much as a hundred and fifty thousand. It worries me, Sam."

"You worry me."

"Every single transaction is going to be monitored. I just don't want you thinking you can feed any of that into this problem without it being noticed. In other words, it goes back to what I said about this being the wrong time to get cute."

Sam Kimber took one long stride, wrapped his big hands around Gus' upper arms and plucked him up off the chair. The glass fell from Gus' numbed hand, and he gave a small sound of pain and surprise. Sam straightened with him and held him suspended in the air, his startled face six inches from Sam's. He heard the creak of Sam's shoulder muscles and saw the cords stand out in Sam's throat. Sam smiled at him and said in a very soft voice, "Now where would I keep money like that?"

"In . . . in a s-safe place. Geez! Let go!"

"Like where?"

"I don't *know*!" Gus said in despair. "Honest to God!"

"I am going to tell you one small thing," Sam said with a deadly precision. "This place is soundproofed. I think you are a liar. I give you one chance to tell me where I kept that money, one specific place, and if you name the wrong place, I am going to break every fat finger on your left hand, one at a time. And then I am going to ask you again."

"We've known each other for . . ."

The iron fingers sank more deeply into his arms. "Be right the first time!"

"For God's sake, Sam! You gave it to Lucille to keep!"

Kimber transfixed him with a look that froze his heart, then abruptly opened the big hands. Gus landed on his heels with such a jar he nipped the tip of his tongue painfully. He sighed and lowered himself to sit on the floor like a fat tired child. His hands were strangely white and completely numb and he could not lift his arms. When he worked his fingers, a painful tingling began.

"Dear God," he muttered and sobbed once, a harsh sound which surprised him.

Sam squatted on his heels and stared into Gus's face. "Let's go into the thing real deep, Mr. G. Real, real deep."

Gus sighed. "I have to protect myself."

"You're next thing to dead this minute, so you better start."

Gus told himself that was a joke, and he looked directly

at Sam to make certain, but that terrible look was still there, and Sam's face was wet and rigid and gray.

Gus swallowed convulsively. "Once I was pretty sure you had cash someplace, I wondered where it would be. You'd know enough not to keep it in lock boxes. I remembered a trip you took without much point to it, and guessed you'd gone and brought it back. I decided you'd hidden it. Maybe here. Maybe at the shack. I thought about that a long time. Honest to God, Sam, it's just that I . . . start wondering about something and I can't rest until I know. It's just the way I am. Then I decided something else. You were so insistent I let you know right away if there was any chance of an indictment for fraud and a chance of federal prison. You're not a man who could stand prison. And you have to make business trips. And you couldn't carry that money around, could you? You'd have to leave it with somebody. Somebody who'd bring it to you if things went real bad. And the more I thought about it, the more sure I was it had to be Lucille. So I figured out something to say to her. If she didn't have the money, it wouldn't mean anything to her. But if she did have it, then I'd know."

"And you just had to know. When did you find out?"

"Three weeks ago, I guess. You'd gone to Tampa. I had an appointment with Doc Nile. I was the only one in the waiting room. I leaned around the little desk and whispered in her ear. I said, 'Hope you've put it in a safe place.' If she'd looked at me confused and asked what, I'd have said I was talking about my file card in Doc's office there. It startled her and her eyes got round and she said, 'Of course, it's in . . . What are you talking about?' But it came too late. I said I was talking about the money. She bit her lip and said you'd told her nobody else knew. The it began to make me nervous, thinking she'd tell you how I trapped her. Then Doc took me and when he was through I waited until she was off and we had some coffee. I told her I was trying to look after your best interests on this tax thing and you were a hard man to work with, the way you keep things to yourself. I told her I had figured out there had to be some cash money somewhere, and she'd seemed the likely one to hold onto it for you in case things went bad for you. She seemed confused about the money. She didn't have any idea of the amount there was, and she thought it had nothing to do with your personal finances."

"So you just had to let her know it was money I was holding out."

"No, Sam! Honest and truly, once I got the drift of what you'd told her about it, I went right along with it. She halfway promised not to mention our little talk. I think she started to get troubled about the money, but then she settled down again. I said I'd worked with you a long time, and the only thing I wanted to do was protect you."

A blue-white flash seemed to originate inside Gus Gable's head. There was a painful ringing in his left ear, blood in his mouth. As he pushed himself back to a sitting position he realized Sam must have struck him. He had not seen the slightest movement before the open-handed blow.

"So you bragged on how smart you were, Gussy. Who to?"

"I didn't say a word! Honest and truly, I didn't say a word to anybody! I was trying to forget it ever happened, because I wanted it all the way out of my mind when I was talking to the people in Jacksonville."

Kimber rose slowly from the tireless squat and looked at Gable. He reached toward Gus with a big hand. Gus flinched back. "Come on, get up," Sam said. Gus took the extended hand. Sam yanked him up so hard Gus's feet left the floor and he took several little running steps to get his balance. He found himself running toward a chair, and made a half turn and fell into it, panting. He took his handkerchief out and mopped his face.

"I say in all sincerity, Sam, in all these five years I've never seen you act . . ."

"I must be a little upset, Gussy."

"You shouldn't knock anybody around this way."

Sam moved closer. "Is that advice?" His color was still odd.

"All I meant was . . ."

"Can't you get one little idea of what this is about, you silly little son of a bitch? Lucille is dead and the money is gone."

Gus formed his lips as though to say something, and then let his mouth sag open. He wiped his face again. "Gone?"

"One hundred and six thousand dollars cash money. Thirty years ago one time I was seven weeks shrimping, and we put into Key West ahead of a blow. A Swede from St. Pete had won all the cash money aboard, eighteen dollars, and he didn't get a quarter mile from the dock afore somebody opened him wide with a fish knife and took it offen him."

"But it doesn't have to mean that . . ."

"What do you think it means?"

"Maybe she just hid it better than you thought, Sam."

"It's gone."

"I . . . I just don't know what to say. It . . . it's a lot of money to lose like that."

"That isn't what I lost."

"I don't see why the two things *have* to be related, necessarily."

"You had to let *somebody* know how cute you were."

"Sam, I swear to God I didn't tell anybody. Maybe . . . maybe *she* told somebody. Maybe she got upset and wanted advice from somebody."

"Because you upset her."

"Sam, I was only trying to do my best for you in the only way I know how."

Kimber studied him and nodded and spoke as though to himself. "You plain wouldn't have the guts to go after it or hire somebody to go after it. But you went behind my back and tricked my woman and upset her."

"Sam, I was only . . ."

"You helped me enough, Gussy. I want every last piece of paper that's got anything to do with me or anything I'm connected with pulled out of your files and turned over to Angie by the close of business tomorrow."

"Now wait a minute!"

"Your lease ends the end of this year, but you'd be better off in your mind if you get yourself out of my building soon as you can find a place to move to."

"Sam, you're not thinking clearly."

"Any time you see me coming down the sidewalk toward you, you cross the street, hear?"

"Listen to me!"

"What have you got to say?"

"You need me, Sam. I can do more for you in a tax way than anybody you could get. I know all the problems first hand. I got a perfect way figured to get you out of the pocket you're in right now. In all honesty, Sam, let me advise you that you shouldn't let emotions get the upper hand. Think this over for a few days. What did I do that was so wrong?"

"Let me walk you out, Gussy."

"You'll think about it?"

"I'm thinking about it right now."

"You don't want to do anything hasty. I mean . . . I could tell the tax people maybe I left something out of the balance sheet. An oversight."

"I'm learning more about you every passing minute, Gussy."

Gus Gable walked toward the door and tensed as Sam put a casual arm across his shoulders. They went into the ante-office. Angie was typing. A man in a pale suit was waiting. Gus started to turn but was held motionless as a big hand clasped the nape of his neck. He caught a glimpse of Angie's startled face before Sam turned him toward the door. "Hold that door open for me, Angie honey," Sam said.

"Don't do anything you'll regret!" Gus said in a thin uncertain voice.

"Or you'll sue," Sam said mildly.

Angie held the door open. Gus knew this could not be happening. It would turn out to be a joke. It couldn't happen, because it would spoil the big deal. Charlie Diller had it all set up.

And suddenly he was being rushed toward the open door. At the last moment something grasped the seat of his pants, yanked his legs back, and he heard a grunt of effort. Then he was sliding along the smooth tile on his belly, past the public elevator, scrabbling at the floor with his bare hands. He piled into the far wall, cracking the top of his head painfully. The door behind him hissed shut. He got up uncertainly. He touched the top of his head and looked at the blood on his fingertips. Suddenly he saw the shape of all his days, saw all of the merciless future. He leaned against the wall, his forehead against the textured paneling, and with no attempt to stifle his sobs, he began to cry.


Sam noticed that when Angie went back to her desk she made a rather wide circle around him, and he felt a distant amusement. "Need us some new tax people, I guess," he said. "Gussy will be sending all the files up tomorrow."

"Yes sir, Mister Sam."

"What's the name of those folks in Orlando? Brewer something?"

"Bruner and McCabe, Mister Sam."

"You get them on over here tomorrow afternoon. They'll come a-running."

"Okay, Mister Sam."

He was suddenly aware of the expressionless composure of the young man in the pale suit. "Now just who the hell is this, Miss Angie?"

"Why this here is that insurance man, name of Mr. Paul Stanial," she said.

"Tell him to come on in," Sam said, and went into his office.

# Seven

"SET," SAM KIMBER said to Stanial. He went to a small executive refrigerator set into the paneled wall. "Join me in a beer, Mister Stanial? One time when I was I guess about twenty-three, I optioned me a real nice piece of grove. Snuck in ahead of some Tampa money only because I'd hunted some with the old boy owning it and he had to sell out and move to a high dry place for a lung trouble. Had to scratch so deep for the option money, I damn near had to get out of the habit of eating. The Tampa boys knew I didn't have a prayer of coming up with the closing money. We did some dickering, and it was dragging on, and I wanted to scare them some. These wall boxes for offices had just come out then. So with maybe eleven dollars in the whole world, I wired that Abercrombie and Fitch to rush one of these boxes to each of them, just a little token of nice treatment. Shook them up good. Man can make a gesture like that maybe has good backing. They made a nervous phone call, and I said I was leaving for California the next day. If it was a dollar around the world, I couldn't got out of sight. So they bought it off me at my price in a big hurry."

He levered the cans open, handed one across to Stanial, sat behind his desk and said, "I don't usually terminate business relationships the way you just seen, Mister Stanial. Now what you got on your mind?"

Paul Stanial went through his insurance routine, the presentation of credentials. Throughout it Kimber watched him idly, and under the sallow brows the eyes were as unemphatic as two bits of watery glass in a taxidermy shop.

"Want to rule out suicide, you say."

"Or establish it, Mr. Kimber."

"Interesting. Now why would you be coming to me?"

"It seems to be common knowledge you were a close friend of the deceased."

"And a thing like you're trying to prove or disprove, you got a natural right to go around asking a lot of real personal questions, I guess."

"Part of the job, Mr. Kimber."

"You good at your job, Mister Stanial?"

"I seem to keep the company satisfied."

"You let me have the policy number, on account of I want to phone up the home office of that North Atlantic Mutual and tell them just how nice and dignified and all you're doing this here unpleasant job."

"I would certainly appreciate that, Mr. Kimber."

"By God, there wasn't one little change in your eyes then. There's one thing I like, it's a man can handle his job. And I don't know as I'd get too much enjoyment out of you in a poker session, Mister Stanial."

"I'm afraid you've lost me, sir."

"You know, you could damn near sell me on this thing. It's just that I happen to know Lucille didn't have any such policy."

"I beg your pardon?"

"Oh, come off it, for crissake! I went over every part of her private financial affairs, Stanial. No two people ever had less secrets. Want me to tell you about her insurance? She had a little two thousand dollar policy she was trying to hang onto with Connecticut General, a straight life policy, and the premium loans had used up about all the little bit of equity she had in it. Her mother is the beneficiary. I tried to talk her into letting me pay it back up to the point where she'd be even with the board, but she wouldn't let me. There was damn little she'd let me do for her."

Stanial waited a long silent moment, then took his legitimate identification card out of his wallet and handed it to Kimber. Kimber examined it and slid it back to him. "Who's paying the freight, Mister Stanial?"

"The sister."

"Why?"

"She thinks Lucille was murdered."

"What gives her that idea?"

Again Stanial hesitated, then opened his brief case and located the photocopy of the significant paragraph of the letter from Lucille to Barbara. Kimber took so long over it, Stanial could not tell how many times he was reading it. Then Kimber finished his beer, wrapped his big right hand around the can and crumpled it as though it were made of foil. He dropped the wadded can in the waste basket beside the desk.

"I am the one she calls A," Kimber said. "And B is the one you seen sliding out on his belly. B is the one tricked her. It would be right nice to know who C is. B tricked her maybe three weeks ago. She should have told me."

"Do you think she was killed, Mr. Kimber?"

"Do you?"

"I stopped playing my games. You want to stop playing yours?"

Kimber swiveled his chair around so far Stanial could see just the back of his neck and left side of his face. "Somehow," Kimber said, "I don't want to say it right out. Even having it in my mind makes me feel as if I'd been gutted. And it gives me a wild feeling back in my head, like if it busted out I'd do terrible things without even knowing I was doing them. When I had my hand on Gus Gable's neck, with Angie going toward the door, I was thinking how easy it would be to turn him the other way and run him right on out that big window over by Mrs. Nimmits' desk, and hear him give one squeak as he dropped into the parking lot. The minute I heard Lu was dead, something died inside me, Mister Stanial. And I just don't give a damn what I do. And that's a dangerous way for a man to be."

"I don't know whether she was killed or not because I don't know what was at stake, Mr. Kimber. I can guess a few things. That position of trust. She was keeping something for you, I guess, because I know you went to her apartment to get it after she died. I don't know what it was, or whether it was still there. You told Mrs. Carey you got what you were after. But I think somebody got there ahead of you."

Kimber whirled the chair back. "Who?"

"I don't know. Whoever took her key. Apparently it was on her key ring with the car keys and two other door keys. And unless somebody took it after it got to Walmo's office, it was taken there at the lake. I know you're in tax difficulties. Walmo seems to think you were after some confidential accounts she was keeping for you."

"Just this minute he stopped having any future in this county."

"He knows who hired me and why. He said he'd stake his life you didn't kill her or have her killed. He believes it was an accidental drowning. But he has to cover himself. Suppose I did come up with some other answer. Then he'd have to explain to the state's attorney why he withheld significant information. Because you're an old friend? His best bet was to level with me."

"Harv just ain't that shrewd, Stanial. He figures I'm down, and down for keeps, so if he stomps me a little, it doesn't matter. You know, maybe he's right."

"How do you mean?"

"If this here turns into an official murder case, it's going to come out what I left with her. And then maybe I am whipped for good."

"What was it?"

"Talking to you like this is part of that not giving a damn any more, I guess. Gus Gable can do me harm, and probably will. What the hell is one more. It was money, boy. Undeclared and unaccounted-for money that just didn't happen to get into the audit they made on me. In a little blue zipper flight bag, packed in solid. One hundred and six thousand dollars cash money."

"Why with her?"

"Why not with her? No matter where I had to run to, I would have sent for her. So it was easier she should bring it, if worse came to worse. Funny thing. By today I would have took it back, on account of the pressure being off. She never did know what it was, Stanial. It was the only time I ever lied to her. And it could have been that lie killed her. I don't know how, but I have that feeling. If I told her what it was she would have thought less of me, and I wanted her to think I was the best man walking. Maybe she wouldn't have held it for me. I don't know. She had strong ideas on the way folks should act. Now I guess I can say it out loud. I think somebody killed Lucille."

"So do I. I think they held onto that key until that night. Mrs. Carey watches a late movie on television every night. The entrance to the apartment is in the back."

"Now hold off there a minute, Stanial. Why would they wait until night? How would they know I didn't have a key to that place, and wouldn't go get it the minute I heard she was dead. I didn't get there until the next day, but how would they be able to count on that?"

"Murderers aren't necessarily logical, Mr. Kimber."

"We better be Paul and Sam, because as of right now we're working the same side of the street. That is, if you're easy in your mind it wasn't me did it or had it done. You could be thinking that way. You could be thinking I get too relaxed with her and tell her too much about some ways I've made money and she gets so upset about it she says she's going to turn me in, and I can't find any other way to stop her."

"I thought of that."

"You'd be damn useless in your work if'n you didn't. Or she was through with me, and I couldn't stand the thought of her going back to that Hanson. And I did get the money back and have it hid. And I had a key all along, but figured it would look better going through Harv Walmo to get it. What you think about that, Paul?"

Stanial opened his notebook, found the right page. "You went to Lakeland that day, Sam. You had an appointment at ten o'clock with a man named Richter and a realtor named Lowe. You examined some property and you had lunch with them, and left the restaurant at two o'clock. It's a fifty minute drive back from there. At about three o'clock, as you were getting out of your car, a man named Charles Best came up to you and told you Lucille had drowned in Flamingo Lake." Stanial closed the notebook. "Hired it done? You'd never give anybody that much leverage to use against you."

"That sister is getting service for her money. I could figure on getting rid of whoever I hired to do it, couldn't I?"

"In that case you'd have thought of a better place than a lake in broad daylight where people might show up at any moment. The circumstances make it look like an impulse killing, Sam."

"But it went off pretty slick. But for that letter to the sister, it would all quiet down."

"Impulse killings sometimes work out as well as the planned ones."

"How about Hanson?"

"I have one more person to see to confirm where he was at the time. Did Lucille have a key to your shack?"

"She had one."

"And one to Doctor Nile's office. But if we assume somebody took the apartment key off the ring, they either had to know what the apartment key looked like or, using a process of elimination, what the other two looked like. They weren't tagged."

There was a knock at the door and Angie Powell opened it. "There anything else for me, Mister Sam?"

"Lord God, girl, it's after seven."

"The league starts at eight tonight. I got time. You want to sign these so they can go out?" She put a thin stack of letters in front of Sam Kimber.

Angie stood beside Sam as he scanned them rapidly, scrawled his name. She smiled absently at Stanial. "Here you go," Sam said. She picked up the letters.

"I got ahold of Mr. McCabe at his home phone," she said. "Him and Mr. Bruner junior can be here at three o'clock tomorrow, if it's okay."

"It'll be all right. You going to miss Gus?"

She looked troubled. "It's not for me to say, Mister Sam. I guess it's whether you will. He did you some good work, it looks like."

"But he messed up on one little thing."

She glanced uneasily at Stanial. "I guess when and if you want to tell me, there'll be a time and place. I just hope he won't . . . find any way to mess us up, Mister Sam."

"He'll sure try."

"Goodnight, Mister Sam. Goodnight, Mr. Stanial."

The monumental girl strode out, silent except for a whisper of fabric, a tick of the door latch, leaving a faint drift of flower perfume in the chilled air.

After a few moments of silence, Stanial said, "I've taken up enough of your time, Sam."

"Hold it a minute. That letter she sent her sister. The way it reads to me, the other person that knew about the money, the one she calls C, they had to find out from Gus."

"It looks that way. But she could have told somebody else too."

"You make out a list of people'd like to do me harm, and you could read yourself to sleep. Then again there would be men who'd see her as tasty, and want to make their try. But she'd battle them. The more you think, the more it widens out, Paul. You think we'll narrow it down?"

Stanial nodded. "Tomorrow people will be talking about murder. And somebody will remember something. It didn't mean anything at the time to them, but they will remember and start wondering, and then tell somebody else. The pressure will build up."

"I'm going to put a little more pressure on Gus. Maybe he let somebody in on it without knowing he was doing it. Could be I could freshen his memory some."

The remnants of the sunset had turned to a dingy saffron, and suddenly it seemed quite dark in the office. A lurid flash of pink lightning was followed immediately by a startling crack and roll of thunder. Kimber stood up and looked out the window, silhouetted, his hands in his hip pockets.

"Working toward it all day," he said.

"Are we going to get it this time?" Stanial asked.

"Going to be a real old soaker."

When the rain became so heavy Stanial could not see to drive, he pulled cautiously off onto the wide soft shoulder and turned the motor off. The rain roared down so heavily onto the car, conversation was impossible. Gusts of wind shook the car. The side vents were the only windows they could leave open. He could see the flashes of lightning but he could not hear the thunder. He thought he heard the girl laugh, a sound of pleasure and excitement. The car windows were opaque with the steam of their exhalations. He lit two cigarettes and handed her one. In the brief illuminations of the lightning he saw her with her back against the passenger door in dark blouse and pale shorts, her young legs curled in the seat. Suddenly the heavy rain turned into a jangling din of hail, and just as suddenly it moved away, leaving them in a relative silence.

"Wow!" the girl said. "Isn't it fantastic?" She hitched around and rolled her window down. "Smell!" she commanded. "The whole world is scrubbed." She opened the door and ducked out into the dwindling rain, scrambled back in with a half handful of melting hail. She slammed the door, and nibbled the hail out of the palm of her small hand. "Lousy sensualist," she said.

"Guess we can be on our way, Shirley."

"It's too nice out to go smell fried food, Mr. Stanial. There's a little state picnic thing up ahead about a quarter mile. Let's stop there."

He found it and parked. The rain had stopped. Fat drops fell from the trees. She sat on the concrete picnic table, her feet on the bench, and commanded him to look up. Half the

sky was black and the other half was bright with stars. The
storm was moving west and they could hear it grumbling into
the distance.

"What I feel toward Kelsey, as I was saying before, is affection," Shirley Feldman said. "I guess it isn't a very com-
plicated emotion. Somebody said he is an empty man but it
isn't that simple, is it?"

"Then what was wrong with the diagnosis?"

"Awareness. That's what's wrong. I'm not a philosophy
major. But I know that one of the things that troubles a lot of
people is this phenomenon of the hollow man in western
culture. Reisman talks about the outer-directed man who
gets his only feeling of substance from conforming to group
standards. So the pathetic guy, the real victim, isn't the one
who can go merrily along with the whole deal, just because
he's been taught to be so damn flexible. The pathetic one is
the guy like Kelse who constantly experiences this sort of . . .
emptiness. I mean he wonders if he shouldn't go sign up
with Schweitzer. It's sort of like the architect in that Graham
Greene book who goes to the leper colony, but he doesn't
know what the hell he's doing there. Of course, the architect
is on a higher level of development than Kelse. Poor Kelse
isn't really a thinking animal. He can follow things up to a
point, and then they get all murky for him and he loses patience with the whole thing. Does it sound too impossible
for me to say I have a much better mind?"

"I imagine you have."

"So I guess he turned into a sort of project for me. You
could say I inherited him from one of my dearest friends.
She gave up on him, completely. I mean she's very sweet but
she decided that he was faking *everything*. And he isn't, of
course. Oh, he fakes a lot, but underneath there is this terrible *concern*. And she misunderstood the sexual urgency.
She thought she was just being *used*. But her own sexual attitudes are very involved and self-conscious. She thinks she
is utterly objective, but the proof is the way she'll go into
screaming fits of rage if you even *look* dubious when she gives
one of her lectures. Kelsey has been a sort of a project because when you find somebody who holds themself absolutely
*valueless*, it's a symptom of a lot of things wrong with our
culture, don't you think? I guess it's like a scientist finding
an absolutely pure strain of some virus. And he lumbers
around with this terrible *guilt*. I feel much older when I'm
with him. And what I was beginning to learn, I guess, is that

you can't try to cure the guilt in anybody. You have to go after their *necessity* to feel guilt. That wife of his was a guilt symbol. Really, I don't think he ever loved her. I don't think Kelsey can genuinely love anybody because he doesn't love himself enough. But she was a symbol of failure."

"Do you think he could have wanted to destroy her, as a symbol?"

"I don't know. It would have been an indication of progress, wouldn't it? I mean he would have been trying to eradicate the necessity to feel guilt. What I was trying to do, mostly, was to prove to him he is quite a nice person underneath, and would be perfectly all right if he stopped moaning and tried to *utilize* himself. He made himself feel guilty and wretched about my girl friend, and he tried to feel guilty about me too. He could not seem to get it through his head that if two people feel affectionate toward each other, they have the right and the responsibility to give each other pleasure. In spite of his apparent sophistication he has a truly sick attitude about sex. My God, most of the heartbreak in the world comes from thinking it's so damned important. No, I guess he wouldn't have wanted to destroy her. Maybe subconsciously, but it would be buried so deep he'd never be able to get at it. He would be a lot more likely to destroy himself. And that's what he's doing of course, in all the slow ways. If he gets in touch with me again, I wouldn't want to hurt him, but really I feel sort of finished with him. I guess I've outgrown him."

"You were with him that day."

"Yes. He came to the library in the morning and I had an eleven o'clock, but I cut the class. My uncle had sent me some wonderful cheese. We went to the boat house and we got there before noon. We had the cheese and crackers and we drank a lot of wonderful Mexican wine. We talked and we made love and then we went out in the sun and fell asleep, up on the top deck. Then Korody came and told him about the phone call. Kelse went darting off and after he was gone, Korody said he thought the wife was dead. Somehow it's made me feel strange ever since. I mean I've felt sort of stupid and middle-class. I'm certainly not ashamed of the relationship with Kelsey. When you're honest about something, you can't be ashamed. I wasn't seduced, certainly. And I wasn't martyring myself. It gave me pleasure too. But it makes me feel odd. Do you understand?"

"Of course."

"You don't say very much do you?"

"As I told you, Shirley, the thing I keep wondering about is whether Mrs. Hanson killed herself. And I wondered if Kelsey had ever said anything to you which might sound as if she was capable of doing that."

"Absolutely no! That woman was entirely satisfied with herself, believe me. God, how I despise those paragons! I don't believe there was a crumb of honesty in her. She married for money, and she wanted to keep poor Kelse in absolute *bondage*. He could approach the shrine once in a while if he was properly humble. And then she would sort of endure his horrid animal appetites. And when poor Kelse went to somebody a little more willing and a little more honest, Lucille got full of outraged virtue and left him. Those monsters never kill themselves, Mr. Stanial. People kill them, and good riddance, but they never do themselves in."

"Would you think somebody killed her?"

"I'd like to think so. She had it all worked out. A nice chunk of alimony or a settlement or something, and then she would marry that Mr. Kimber. But I guess she just happened to drown somehow."

"Have you seen Kelsey since?"

"Just for a moment at the funeral to tell him I was sorry. And he looked at me as if he'd never seen me before. I guess he's gone back to his buddies. He hasn't come near the College. He's probably stoned all day long. Poor guy. Now you can take me downtown and feed me, Mr. Stanial. I'm absolutely famished. You know, ever since I began to feel odd about Kelsey, I've been hungry all the time, and I'm getting immense. It might be some sort of compensation, but I can't figure out what it is. I'll have to *really* think about it. Everything is really the pursuit of self-knowledge, don't you think? My God, if this is a guilt reaction, I'll never forgive myself."

The sky was brighter and his eyes were adjusted to the faint light. Under the big dark hairdo and the tousle of bangs, her small face peered out at him like some cautious creature under a bush. At the moment she looked heartbreakingly young, and her voice was uncertain. But that same light of the sky touched the bare mature legs, their compact and sinewy curvatures. They send you up in those things, he thought, before you have a license to fly.

There were an even dozen people at the Keaver party, including the Keavers, and Barbara observed that sometimes it seemed like a great deal more and sometimes it seemed like a great deal less. At the Keaver's lakefront house the ubiquitous screened cage had its long dimension parallel to the lake shore, forming a link between an ornate garden house of Chinese motif and the older boat house. A good half of the floor area of the cage was taken up by a rather shallow swimming pool.

She was able to re-identify the ones she had met, the ones Lucille had mentioned most often in her letters, the Keavers, the Yates, the Bryes. There was an older couple, George and Nina Furrbritt, and another couple the same age as the inner circle, named Coop and Sis Toombs.

The party had a curious resonance, a cyclical swing. It began sedately enough, and with all the polite words of sympathy she had anticipated. But in much less than an hour the weight and the velocity of the drinks had fragmented it into a noisy, hippety-hoppety carnival of pet tricks, interruptions, imitations, inside jokes and meandering slapstick, with twelve people sounding like fifty. Barbara soon realized she had lost her chance to steer the general conversation into speculation about murder. There was no general conversation. You exchanged loud fragments with people who swooped by. And so, when she was handed an exceptionally virulent drink apparently meant for someone else, a vast martini in a tall water glass, she gave an inward shrug and told herself it could be used as a prop. A girl who had sipped her way through one of these could be forgiven for a certain lack of tact. Were she to wobble up to people one at a time and ask them if they thought her sister had been murdered, people would humor the poor creature. And the wobble would be half contrived and, with this drink, half genuine.

As she was convinced the party was going to disintegrate entirely, the great storm came tumbling down upon them and all essential gear was clumsily manhandled into the garden house. The cooperative efforts induced a simulated sobriety. Bonny Yates gave a vivid scream of terror at each flash of lightning. The big grill was partially protected by the roofed portion of the cage, and soon they were all in the garden house, eating mounds of garlic salad out of individual teak bowls, and ravenously devouring the tender slabs of semi-raw beef, amid a half dozen simultaneous conversations conducted in loud voices over the din of the storm. By then

Barbara had used her gambit on four or five people, without any discernible effect, not even surprise, much less the expected shock and consternation. It seemed as though she was asking about some historical figure who had come to grief in the fifth century. As the rain began to dwindle and a torpor of filled bellies began to reduce the volume and the number of the conflicting conversations, there came one spectacularly savage flash-bang which added several screams to Bonny's, and the lights dimmed and went out. All the lights —cage lights, pool lights, landscape lights, garden-house lights, boat-house lights. Amid the renewed whistling of the wind was a primitive, night-charged excitement, a stirring and hooting of the people, and when Barbara started to get up from a footstool, someone moving rapidly by bumped her solidly and sent her floundering into the arms of someone else. The someone else took her commandingly by the arm and led her out of the confusion to the roofed part of the cage and over to one side, into a leafy corner semi-screened by the broad wet leaves of monstera and dwarf banana. The someone put his hands on her shoulders and said, "Out of the paths of restless natives, my dear, and into a bower of total conservatism."

There was just enough faint light to confirm her memory of the voice. George Furrbritt, the older man, a mannered, neat-boned man, with curly cap of gray, yacht-basin tan, and a look of humorous, self-effacing slyness. His wife was Nina, the rangy busty redhead with the macaw voice and the exaggerated mouth mannerisms of one who speaks only for lip-readers.

Barbara wanted to say words of thanks to match the ornateness of his remark, but heard herself say, in a tone of complaint, "Nobody will talk about my sister being murdered." She knew she was drunk, and afflicted with the single-minded purpose of a drunk.

"I will talk about anything in the world you wish to talk about, my dear." He held her by the upper arms and kissed her on the mouth, not long enough to make her object, and with a quiet and casual authority which would have made objection seem inane. "Let us examine it as a reasonable conjecture."

"You think it is? Reasonable?"

"We start with the assumption the world of Sam Kimber is more violent and primitive than this one. And that's the world she was in." He kissed her again, with a more masterful insistence, and she felt that the kisses were the price of this talk in the rainy darkness.

"Why is it more violent?" she asked when her mouth was free, and she had the feeling her voice had come loose somehow, come adrift, separate and murmurous. And she thought that the darkness things do not count because no one can see.

"Oh, because of money and deals, and maybe the kind of people in Kimber's world. Does it matter so much?" And with a dancer's deftness, he pivoted her around, bumped her softly back against the redwood wall, held her more intimately and worked at her mouth with a curiously indifferent insistence, and a gourmet precision.

She realized vaguely that she should have said no, but somehow the place for no had been too quickly passed, like turning two pages at once in a book and losing track. She was bemused, remote, half-dreaming, yet making her responses to him as she wondered mildly who could have guessed that he would be so good and so absolutely sure and knowing about these little good-feeling things and ways, turning it into a kind of a joke you are playing on the world, because really things do not start this way, and soon it will have to be stopped, but how do you stop it when it seems as if it would be some sort of strange social error to end it with less social grace than he is making it happen with. More knowing than Roger, even, and so absolutely certain. . . .

Mingled in the growing blood-roar in her ears she heard the meaningless festival of darkness around her, the yelps and laughings, a rip of fabric, slap of flesh, coy squeal of a faked indignation. She felt as if she were slowly being opened outward, and now his mouth was tracing her throat, while her head lolled and smiled to the increased chuffing of her breath, and she was so suffused in recurrent waves of bonelessness she felt herself sagging, and was but remotely, unimportantly, mildly astonished to feel that he had somehow and cleverly bared her left breast, lifting it to a knowing caress.

Abruptly all the lights came on and her dazed eye caught a photographic image of the pool people, saw it all in a moment of subjective frozen silence, saw naked Nina Furrbritt on the apron of the pool, teetering off balance, all naked pipestem legs and schoolboy hips and great implausible sallow melony breasts, saw the satyr bareness of Coop Toombs who had just pushed her, saw the abandoned party clothing in damp heaps, saw the great bobble and thrash of breasts and bellies and buttocks and wet grimacing faces in the wrestling game in the shallows of the pool. Time began again and the woman fell, and Coop Toombs dived after her, and there were yelps of dismay and derision at the sudden exposure. The hostess eeled quickly out of the pool and headed in a nude, awkward run toward the control panel for the lighting. Barbara shoved Mr. Furrbritt away from her and hitched her sheath top back up onto her left shoulder. The lights began to go out as the hostess tweaked the panel controls, amid cheers of approval.

Furrbritt moved in upon her again and she knocked him back with her forearm across his throat.

"The boat house!" he said irritably.

"What?" she asked blankly.

"The boat house! The loft, my dear child!" he cried ir- ritably and grabbed her wrist. She snatched it away. In the faint light of the faraway outside floods the hostess had left burning, Mr. Furrbritt seemed to be doing a small, nervous, hoppity dance, all his casual authority forgotten. He snatched her wrist with greater strength and began dragging her along, and suddenly she was terrified.

With her free hand she hit George Furrbritt solidly on the nape of the neck. He spun and hissed at her and slapped her sharply across the face. Suddenly Kelsey Hanson loomed between them, clothed and sullen. He turned a broad back toward Barbara and made a small pivoting motion. There was a quick wet sound, not loud, but inexpressibly ugly. All the tidy, neat-boned confidence of Mr. Furrbritt dropped into the soaked peat moss of a planting area, and on the way down his head rang the reflector of a stake light like a gong. Han- son turned and grabbed her arm and yanked her away, led her around the busy pool, out a screened door, across an area of wet grass and into the mouth of a narrow wet woodsy path. She fought him, but he did not even seem to realize she was struggling. Wet leaves soaked her clothing. "You were right, Lucille," Kelsey Hanson said. "Oh you were so damn right, Lu, honey. They're lousy people and I should have listened to you. We're going home where you belong, sweetheart."

# Eight

THE LEAGUE was scheduled at eight o'clock. Angie Powell arrived so late that by the time she had changed her shoes, she had time for just one practice ball. She was anchor man on the girls' Kimberland team, with a 178 average. They were scheduled on lanes eleven and twelve. It annoyed her. She never did well on eleven. It was slightly tacky, just enough to pull her into a fat hit and too many baby splits.

She smiled and nodded and spoke to all the friends who greeted her. She wore white elk-hide shoes, white wool ankle socks, a short white pleated tennis skirt, a sleeveless white blouse with Kimberland written across the back in blue embroidered script. She had embroidered it herself, making it at the same time larger and more ornate than the stenciled ones. She wished she could write Kimberland on everything she wore.

The ball she owned was white. Inside the finger holes it was Chinese red. It was as heavy as most men used. She had worked carefully on her style to take maximum advantage of her height and strength. She took four steps and a long slide, starting the delivery with a slow push-away. At the end of the delivery she brought her right hand up sharply. It was a fast ball with a small quick hook into the pocket at the end of it. As she delivered the ball, she felt fleet and strong and precise. It had pleased her to be told she bowled like a man. But several months ago a friend had taken movies of her delivery, and she had been disappointed to see how she looked. There was far too much bounce of golden curls and girlish undulation of hip on the way to the line and, in the profile shots, too much flounce of breasts. So she had taken to binding her hair with a white ribbon, wearing a sturdier bra, consciously controlling her hip movement.

Midway through the first game she knew she was in trouble. She had one clean miss of the ten pin and two splits she had been unable to pick up. With the self-knowledge of the natural athlete, she knew that the flaw was in her concentration. Too many random things were intruding—the look on Gus's face just before Mister Sam had slid him down the hall, the way Mister Sam looked and acted, the chance Gus would make trouble.

She pushed everything out of her mind except the clean mechanics of the delivery, and the variable geometry of the maple pins. Her team sagged with her and they lost the first game by over eighty pins. She had her first frame on lane eleven in the second game. She decided to adjust to the alley by giving the ball a little more speed, but without losing control at the top of the backswing. As it went down she saw it would be too thin, but at the final instant it ducked into the pocket and the picture strike cleared the lane completely. She spun and jumped into the air, clapping her hands, beaming at her teammates. She put four strikes together, and ended with 211 for the second game, which they won by sixty pins. They won the third game by forty pins, enough for the match, and she computed her average for the evening at 184.

Linda had to hurry home. So the four remaining teammates went to Ernie's Place for the usual Po' Boy sandwiches. Alma's boy picked her up there. Jeanie and Stephanie kept trying to pump Angie about what had happened between Mister Sam and Gus Gable. She concealed her irritation with them. There was no reason for them to know anything about it. They just worked there. They didn't know what loyalty meant, really. They just wanted something to talk about.

Stephanie had brought Jeanie in her car. Angie walked out with them as though to get into her little gray Renault and go home, but as soon as they drove out, she went back into Ernie's and went to the phone booth and called Gus' office number. It rang eight times, then ten. As she decided to let it ring fifteen, Gus answered.

"It's Angie, Gus. Angie Powell. I thought you'd be working."

"You mean you know why I'd be working."

"I guess so. One of the things I wanted to say, you should have most of the files upstairs before three tomorrow."

"Who's taking over?"

"I couldn't tell you that, Gus."

"I swear to you, he was like a crazy man! There's no rhyme or reason to it. Throwing me . . . literally *throwing* me out! You were there. Did you ever see anything like that in your life?"

"Never, Gus. Never. Honest, he hasn't been himself since she died."

"That's for sure."

"But he'll be himself again a little later on."

"Too late for me, though."

"That depends."

In a more cautious tone he said, "What do you mean by that, Angie?"

"I shouldn't be talking to you at all."

"So?"

"But you've been so much help to him. I know he needs you."

"Sure. Try to tell him that."

"I did try to tell him that."

"Thanks, Angie. Keep trying."

"I guess it's more like it's up to you. I mean if you want to work for him after what he did."

"I want to work for him. I don't get hurt feelings that easy, believe me."

"Well . . . I have some ideas."

"Like what?"

"You sound eager enough, Gus. But I couldn't tell you like this, over the phone. And I don't feel right about seeing you."

"Why not?"

"Somebody might see us together. And that wouldn't look right if Mister Sam heard about it. The state he's in, he might not understand at all that I'd see you only to try to help him. I don't give a darn about you, Gus. You know that. I just want for Mister Sam to have the best possible help in his troubles."

"Nobody has to see us together."

"And you wouldn't tell anybody you were meeting me."

"No."

"Then have you got any ideas?"

"You could come to my place, maybe?"

"Oh, no. I couldn't do that, Gus."

"Sam wants to see me. He phoned. He sounds meaner than ever. He hasn't cooled off a bit."

"What does he want to see you about?"

"He didn't say."

"Did you agree to see him tonight?"

"No. He's just not ready to talk sensibly. If you've got any ideas on how to handle him, truthfully I would appreciate it with all my heart."

"I have to go on home now because Mama always waits up. But I could sneak back out again. If we could just ride around a little bit in your car I could tell you what I think. Maybe it would work and maybe it wouldn't. Anyhow, if a little after midnight, you could park over on Tyler maybe, next to the furniture place that burned down, it's just back across lots for me."

"I know where you mean. Angie, I do appreciate this."

"Maybe there's nothing I *can* do, Gus."

"But to tell the truth I am pleased by your willingness to try."

"It's just that it's best for Mister Sam."

"Of course, dear."

As she was walking out of the place Ernie stopped her and said, "You know my kid sister, Pam. Well, she got admitted to Gainesville the way she wanted, but now she's got the idea she should go to business school, and I was wondering about that place you went to in Orlando, Angie."

Angie Powell gave the problem her complete attention. "Gee, I don't know as it would be so good, a girl not having a place to stay, like I was at my aunt's."

"You think she'd get much out of it?"

"I guess it would be how hard she wanted to work at it, Ernie. I mean they can teach you if you want to work at it. I went there first to learn nursing."

"I didn't know that, Angie."

"Oh sure. I was going to be a medical missionary. I was good on the class work, learning the anatomy and all, but it turned out I got a weak stomach. Anything bloody and I'd fall over like a tree. So I changed to secretarial."

"But it's a good school."

"Sure is, Ernie, that is if you want to work."

"I don't know as Pam wants to work at anything. Say, I got the twin speedometers checked out and I can hold it right on the button now. How about coming out Sunday? We're going to set the gates up and run slalom all day long."

She looked at him sternly. "Ernie, you know better than that!"

He snapped his fingers. "Sunday. I forgot, Angie."

"Any other day you can make it, Ernie, real early or after work."

"I'll let you know."

She drove home. The pavement was dry but there were puddles in the gutters. She put her noisy little gray Renault in the back yard and went in through the kitchen carrying her bowling kit. Her mother sat in her reinforced chair at the kitchen table pasting green stamps in booklets. Mrs. Powell was a huge woman, almost as tall as Angie and grotesquely fat. The flesh of her ankles hung over the sides of her shoes. Her small and bitter mouth was tucked back behind her pendulous cheeks. Her nose was small and thin. She had the same odd and beautiful eyes as her daughter, an unusual lavender-blue, but her lashes were stubby and the whites of her eyes were muddy. In spite of her weight, Mrs. Powell was an active woman, participating in every aspect of church work, full of rancor and suspicion, responding with a notorious violence to every fancied slight, mercilessly castigating a sinful world. Her subdued little husband, Jimmy Powell, had worked behind the scenes in the post office for twenty-six years.

Mrs. Powell looked at her daughter from head to toe with a vivid animosity. "I can tell you, Angela, it is a thankless job for me to be head of the committee on clean reading and spend a whole afternoon like I done today weeding out the naked Communist filth down to the court house newsstand and then have you prancing around alone in the nighttime in a little skirt halfway up to your crotch."

"Oh, Mama, please. I've told you and told you that . . ."

"You always tell me that when you go swimming you wear considerable less. And I suppose if you went walking and come onto a nudist camp, you'd strip everything off and parade yourself around jaybird naked just because everybody else is. I tried to raise you a decent Christian girl, and you go a-flaunting your body around raising dirty thoughts in the minds of men."

"Mama, I can't be responsible for what other people think."

"And you come in here twenty minutes late, talking sassy to your mother, and how am I to know you haven't been out squirming around in the bushes, doing the devil's work, abandoning yourself to the pleasures of the flesh?"

"Mama, I went to Ernie's with Alma and Jeanie and Stephanie and had a sandwich like always, and maybe we talked a little longer than usual."

"A lot of dirty talk?"

"Mama!"

"I know what those office girls are like. Don't you tell me!"

"We won, Mama."

"Again? That's wonderful, dear."

"I got two-eleven in the middle game, and Jeanie did

better than she ever did before." She yawned, muffling it with
her fist. "I'm pretty tired, Mama. You don't have to worry
about me." She went around the table and kissed the great
slab of cheek. "I'll never in my whole life do anything to
make you ashamed."

"You're a good girl, Angie. It's just I worry about you. The
devil waits around every turn. A man will say sweet words to
you, but if you should listen, you soon find out that the only
thing he ever did have on his mind was to get you over
onto your back and have his dirty way with you. That's
the way the world is, ever since we were flang out of the
Garden. I'm not a selfish woman. I've told you a hundred
times I can get along having no grandchildren on account of
it would mean selling you off into the vile bondage of marriage where a woman has no rights at all and is turned into
a soiled vessel for the brute pleasure of some dirty-minded
man, crying herself to sleep night after night after he's shamed
her and sickened her."

"You don't have to worry, Mama. I'd rather be dead."

"That's my sweet Angie."

Angie Powell showered quickly and did her exercises in
her cotton pajamas and went to bed. After fifteen minutes she
got up and went silently to the open door of her mother's
room. She listened for a full minute to the cadence of the
soft rumbling snores. She paused outside her father's closed
door, but could hear no sound. Back in her own room, she
changed quickly and silently to her gray twill coveralls and
blue sneakers. She tied a scarf around her hair, shoved a
pair of cotton gloves into her pocket and went out her bedroom window. She lowered herself to the grass. The screen
was hooked at the top. She let it swing silently back into
place. She stayed in the shadows. To get through to Tyler
Street, she had to cross the playground of Southwest School.

As she was skirting the playground, she had a sudden
hearty impulse, and after making certain she was not observed, she went over to the swings, grasped the slanted pipe
support, took a deep breath, and then went swiftly up, hand
over hand. When she neared the top of the inverted V, she
reached out and snatched the other support with her right
hand, then hung there for a moment, feeling the good pull
of the muscles across her back. She let go, dropped, landed
lightly, sitting on her heels for a moment, fingertips against
the ground for balance.

She stood up. She stood with her legs apart, hands on her

hips. She felt all rared back within herself, high-chested and immune. She had her Joan-feeling, the stake, the smile, the armor, the curved pattern of the flames. And it was mixed with the red mare-feeling, the one that made her arch her back and stick her buttocks out. Neat hooves to chop the meadow grass, and a small pleasant sweat of exertion, and the ability to shiver any portion of the roany hide to dislodge the hungry fly.

Gus was parked in the driveway near the blackened shell of the furniture store. He was standing beside the dark car. She saw the red glow of his cigar. It amused her to circle him and come up behind him and stand there for a long time, just looking at him. She touched him on the shoulder. He bleated and leaped and whirled and gasped, "Jesus Christ!"

"Apologize to God," she said sternly.

"What?"

"That was blasphemy, Gus."

"Oh. Well. I'm sorry."

"Don't tell me."

"God, I'm sorry. Amen. I can tell you sincerely, Angie, you nearly stopped my heart."

She saw a late car coming down Tyler, and she moved to keep Gus' car between her and the moving car until it had passed.

"What's the matter with you, Angie?"

"I told you. Suppose somebody told Mister Sam I saw you tonight?"

"I suppose. How do you handle Sam? He does his share of cussing."

"Not in front of me. Not ever. He knows it irks me."

"Well, did you say we could drive around?"

"Come to think of it, we could just as well talk here. I guess I'd feel better. Let's walk around in back."

Far across the flat marshy land behind the cinderblock shell, she could see the moving lights of traffic on Route 27. A pile of lumber covered with building paper was stacked five feet high against the rear wall of the building. She jumped lightly up and sat and gave Gus her hand. He climbed up with the aid of a cinderblock on edge.

He sighed and said, "I can tell you in all honesty, Angie, I've never felt so terrible about anything in my life. I mean it was always a business relationship and nothing social on the side to speak of, but after five years you get the feeling there is a relationship aside from business. I have had no one lay hands on me in violence since I was a schoolboy, and the shock of it made me nauseous all day. Even allowing for a great tragedy coming into his life, it seems that he would do a thing like that . . . with more taste, not in front of you and a stranger."

"I guess you made him awful mad, Gus."

"It was a business thing, but he took it in a personal way. I don't know what makes you think you can make him feel better toward me."

"If I can't, what will you do?"

"Angie, I just don't know. I keep thinking I have to think of myself. How can I survive in my business with people knowing about it? Like a damn fool I went downstairs, bleeding, and so confused I told the people in my office what happened. It's all over town. How can I hold onto the clients I've got left? What I could say, Sam wanted me to do something crooked on this tax compromise and I refused and he threw me out."

"That would be a lie, Gus."

"I've got a business to protect. How much should I protect a man who slides me out the door? And I've got to think of the Jacksonville contacts too. I can do a good job for my clients because I'm respected. He should have thought of all these things before he laid hands on me. If you can fix it, it will be good for Sam and good for me."

"I have some ideas, but I have to know a little more about what you quarreled about."

Gus bit the tip off a fresh cigar and spat it into the darkness. "He wanted me to do a perfect job for him without telling me the whole story. If he'd told me, would I have to find out my own way? Then he gets sore. Was she some kind of a princess or something?"

"Gus. Was he really sore because he thought that after you found out, you might have told somebody else?"

"Truthfully, I swore up and down I had not so much as opened . . ." He stopped and turned his head and looked at her. "You sound like you know a lot about it already."

"Maybe I find out things my own way."

"Like what?"

"Like I wondered why you spent so much time going back over those old personal records. You wouldn't take them out of the office, and you'd work on them when Mister Sam was on trips. You made out it was part of the tax case, but you were looking back before the years they were interested in.

And you wouldn't take them down to your own office. It just seemed funny, Gus. You ran tapes and threw them in my basket. And you wrote figures down and balled them up and threw them in my basket. I wondered if I ought to speak to Mister Sam about it. You acted sneaky, Gus, I swear."

"Just doing my job."

"I saved those tapes and pieces of paper and they sure puzzled me, Gus. Then one day I got it figured out. You were taking everything he took in, and then subtracting the taxes he paid and subtracting all the estimated personal money you figured he spent, and subtracting the net worth off the balance sheet, to find out if there was something left you didn't know about."

"You're a bright girl, Angie."

"You know, I don't think I would have got onto it if you hadn't said something funny to me a month ago. You said it like a joke and then you looked at me real close, but it wasn't a joke, was it?"

"What did I say to you?"

"Why, Gus, you should remember! You said I was about as good as a bank except I didn't pay any interest. I just didn't know what in the wide world you were talking about. Later on, that's what started me thinking about cash money, and figuring out that's what you were looking for. But you hadn't figured out where it was. Next chance I had, I searched all through Mister Sam's apartment. You know what I found? A suitcase in the closet all packed, and him without a trip in sight. Clothes to last quite a spell, Gus. But no money. Then something else scared me."

"What?"

"A passport with his picture in it, but it was a different name. And some business papers and things to match up with the new name. And thirty-five thousand dollars in bearer bonds. And a skinny green bank book without a name, just with French printing on it, from a bank in Zurich, showing twelve thousand pounds in that bank."

"So my top guess was closer."

"But no money. And it was the next day I asked you if he was in bad trouble."

"I told you the truth, Angie. I said that if they indicted him for fraud, I did not see how they could make it stick. I thought it would be a mistake on their part. But no trial is ever a sure thing, and there would always be the off chance he might have to do a year in Atlanta. But as it turned out, it was all worked out very smoothly."

"That's the kind of chance Mister Sam would never take. When they come to get him, he'd be long gone. I suppose if you told them all this stuff, they'd come down on him again, rougher than before."

"Not if there's any chance of our settling our differences."

"Gus, I just don't see how you're going to do that. Because the truth of the matter is that if you hadn't started getting so sneaky, and making that fool joke, I wouldn't have figured out about the money and who had it. When I talked to her to make sure of it, she thought you'd told me. And I guess you did without knowing it. Mister Sam has a weakness for women, but I can't say it's pure evil. They lead him on and he can't help himself sometimes."

"You talked to her?"

"And I lied to her, but it was in a good cause. I went quiet to her place one night, and she let me in all silk and lace and perfume. I told her I knew she had the money and she said she did. I called her a wicked fornicator. Then I told her the lie. I told her that you were planning to turn Mister Sam in so you'd get a percentage on the tax, and to say nothing to Mister Sam because he'd do some wild, crazy thing that would get him in worse trouble. I said you'd promised me you'd wait a while, and I was figuring out a good way to stop you, but I thought I'd need her help, and I'd let her know."

He was looking at her. His face was a featureless blur in the starlight, except for the vague calligraphy of the dark frames of his glasses.

"He sure wasn't going to run off, not even alone," she continued. "I protect that man with all my heart and soul, Gus. I'm not going to let another thing hurt him, all the rest of his life. Nothing. Nobody." She realized that Gus, moving ever so slowly, had hitched forward and was reaching a questing toe down toward the cinder block.

"So," she said, "with her being alive today if it wasn't for you getting sneaky, I can't see Mister Sam ever feeling kindly toward you."

As he started to lunge toward escape, she swiveled on her seat and snapped her long legs out and caught him between them, locked toe and ankle. Her legs were diagonally around his chest, pinning one arm. His feet were on the ground and his struggles threatened to drag her off the lumber pile. She rolled face down and hooked her fingers onto the back of

the pile. He was making breathy gasping sounds and scrabbling weakly at the tough twill with his office fingers. She
slowly increased the pressure, feeling the thews and tendons
of her long round golden legs turn as solid as marble.

Abruptly he slumped. She held his weight for a few more
moments, then let him drop. She eased herself down to stand
straddling him, and put on the white cotton gloves. She bent
and laid her hand against his throat and felt the fast, ragged
cadence of his breathing. She lifted him and held him pinned
against the lumber, then dug her right shoulder into the pit
of his stomach and let him fall forward across her strong
back. When she was properly braced and balanced, her right
arm hugging his slack legs, she stood up with a single powerful effort. She walked with her knees locked, taking short
steps. With each step a swinging hand casually patted the
back of her thigh. When she reached the car she opened the
door on the driver's side with her left hand. With another
quick and violent effort she lowered him and pushed him in
onto the seat. As he toppled over onto his back, his elbow
touched the horn ring, startling her briefly. She looked in all
directions, her head tilted, listening. She bent and picked his
heavy legs up and put them inside, his feet by the pedals. She
leaned in and hooked her hand around the nape of his neck
and pulled him into proper position behind the wheel. She
guided him cautiously as he slumped forward. But the motion
stopped before he reached the horn ring. He sat puddled in
upon himself, chin on his chest, making a mild snoring
sound.

She could not get at him the way she had planned. She
had to change position and kneel beside the car, half facing
him as she pulled off her right glove. She reached across him
with her left hand and grasped his right shoulder, held it to
steady him. She dug her right hand, hard fingers extended,
into the softness of his diaphragm on his left side, above the
spongy mass of belly, just under the hard ridge of the
lowest rib. The sport shirt was making it more difficult.
She unbuttoned it and pulled it out of the way, then again
socketed her fingers deeply into softness, reaching up
under the edge of rib. The flaccidity repelled her. She
strained but felt she could not reach far enough. She braced
her shoulder and then felt something give, some soft tearing
of inner tissues. Gus Gable groaned and stirred.

"Easy now," she whispered. "Not long now, not long at all."

The hard edge of rib was now against the pad at the base

of her thumb, her hand deep into the huddled man. And she felt it move against her fingers, the warm beating muscle, big as two clenched fists, working in a rubbery way against the pads of her index and middle fingers.

This was the depth and the essence of Gus. She waited and suddenly she had the Joan-feeling, the flames hot against her face and body. And the red mare feeling mixed with it. Her hand was beginning to cramp with the effort, but she endured it. He moved. With a great effort she forced her thumb away from her fingers then gave a deep, prodding, savage tweak. The heart leaped and fluttered and she pressed it into silence. It was as before. Gus gave a curiously prolonged tremor. Not quite a shudder. He made a remote gagging, rattling sound. And wave upon wave of a delicious burning feeling shook her and weakened her as she yanked her hand down and out of the deep socket which disappeared instantly. She sat back on her haunches for several seconds, her eyes closed, breathing through her mouth, then quite briskly buttoned his shirt and replaced the right glove. She closed the car door and got in on the other side. She pushed the body over against the door, hitched close to him and started the car. She could see no lights in either direction. She put the automatic shift in low and the car crept out of the drive. She turned it north, away from the school. She put it into drive and it moved at a reasonably fast walk. She aimed it down the middle of Tyler Street, put the lights on, stepped out and slammed the car door. She ran into the schoolyard shadows and stood behind a tree and watched it. After several dozen yards it began to angle toward the right. It bumped the curb and the impact turned the wheels. It angled across the road to the left. She ran a hundred feet and stopped and held her breath and listened. She heard it going through the heavy brush with a sound like somebody crackling thick paper. Then there was a thud and the crackling stopped. But the motor was still running. She could hear it.

She was in bed when she heard the siren. It droned down to a growl that died away nearby. It did not start up again. There was no need for haste. She thought of the bruise. If they wondered about it, they would think the edge of the steering wheel had done it. And if, when she had clenched all the strength of her legs around him, she had cracked any ribs, it would make no difference whether they found them or not.

When she was quite certain they were gone and had taken him away, she got up in the darkness. Her room was small and plain. She eased open the bottom drawer of her bureau and lifted out the shallow box of wooden beads. She put it on the floor in front of the window and set the lid aside. She rolled her pajama legs above her sturdy knees, then knelt upon the colored beads, slowly transferring her weight, then straightening, kneeling erect, her palms pressed together in the old gesture of prayer. The agony grew, and she accepted it because it would free her. Just as it began to reach the limit of her endurance, she felt a strange swarming and shifting of a darkness behind her eyes. Her lips had a numbed, tingling feeling. Her breathing slowed and deepened, and her eyelids fluttered. The pain faded away, and she knelt on a feathery softness. Thus was the pain to Joan too, the flames as nothing, the smile, the prayer and the answer.

She did not have to say the words, or think the words. They moved across the blackness behind her eyes. "I am Thy virgin warrior, Thy pure sword of justice. Give me the proper humility to do Thy work. I have slain the whore and the money changer, doing Thy bidding. But I do not have the purity of Saint Joan. Another thing comes into my mind, and I do not know if it is a wickedness. Help me. I should not take such a hot sweet pleasure in doing Thy work. It is an arrogance. It should be done coldly and sadly, with prayers for their souls. But I forget the prayer. Test me. Use me. Teach me. Forgive me."

She slowly stretched her arms out at her sides, horizontal, palms upward. She tilted her head back. In a furrier blackness she willed a total rigidity. It began with her fingers, turning them hard and numb, and she felt it spread up her arms as her breathing became even slower. It locked her shoulders and spread down her back and down across her belly, drawing all the fibered muscles to an iron rigidity, slowly turning haunch, flank, thigh, calf to tireless stone. And as her throat and face began to harden, and she began to slide into the greatest blackness of all, she said hastily to herself, in a tiny inward voice, "One hour."

She came out of the blackness and felt the simultaneous softening of all her muscles. Her arms drifted down to her sides, and at the first warning of discomfort she stood up. She felt dazed and soft, rested and refreshed. She put the shallow box of beads away. She got into her bed and rolled the pajama legs down. The flesh of her knees was dimpled by the long cruel pressure, but she was without pain. She had learned it when she was fifteen, had read of Joan and wept and tried to hold her arm over a candle flame and could not, and wept again because she was unworthy. She had tried many times, and one night she had tried holding her arm high over the flame and slowly bringing it down, as slow as the minute hand of a clock. And that night she had found the secret of making the blackness come, of turning flame into a gentle kiss, turning the stink of searing flesh into a smell of flowers—the secret of Joan. But there were too many burns to hide, too many little hard white scars on the underside of her right arm. She experimented and found the beads would do as well, and she had used them for eight years. They were the proof that, among all the millions, she had been chosen.

As she crossed the edge of sleep, the hidden heart began to pump against her hand, but this time her hand slid through to where she could grasp it completely, and as she did so, she burst out of sleep to discover herself suffused with the red mare feeling, her back powerfully arched, her breath fast and shallow, her skin tingling, her loins hollow, her nipples engorged and painfully sensitive. She turned onto her back and her body slowly quieted. She flexed her right knee, clenched her fist and struck herself on the top of the thigh as hard as she could, three times. And then she began to wonder who would next be pointed out to her. She wondered what she would do if it should be Mister Sam. She wondered if she would have the strength and the will to do it. He was a sinner, but soon he would be beyond the wickedness of the flesh, and then he would see the Truth and it would bring him to his knees, begging forgiveness. She would kneel beside him and tell him what must be said.

Planning the words she would teach him, she sank once again into the deep, gentle and trusting sleep of the totally healthy creature in the first rich years of its physical maturity.

# Nine

PAUL STANIAL heard the night-drone of the air-conditioner as he went silently and warily up the first flight of steps at the Hanson boat house. When he reached the level of the covered deck, he peered in. There was a single lamp lighted. The semi-opaque shade was blue. He thought he could make out a figure on the bed.

"Paul?" an uncertain voice said, off to his right. He turned quickly. Barbara Larrimore got out of a deck chair and came tentatively toward him, and when he spoke her name, she hurried the rest of the way, lurching solidly and rather clumsily against him.

He put his arms around her and said, wonderingly, "Your clothes are all damp."

She made a muffled sound that could have been sob or laugh. "They were worse," she said in a low voice. "I've dried off some. Dear God, what an absolute nightmare evening." She stepped back away from him. "I'm sorry. Weakened condition. But not drunk. I was, for a while."

"You sounded so strange over the phone."

"It's near the bed and the last thing I wanted to do was wake him up. Paul, *please* take me away from here. I called three times . . ."

He walked toward the stairs with her. "It was ringing when I came in. Have you got everything? Purse?"

"I left it somewhere, and if they have another room key for me, I couldn't care less. I'm so *damned* ashamed of myself." They reached ground level and he took her arm to guide her along the path. "The thing is, Paul, these people aren't monstrous degenerates. They're just silly. Silly, vulgar show-offs. There's something pathetic about them. They try so hard. And I had to get just as silly as the rest of them. I'll tell you all, as penance."

"You don't have to."

"It will be good for me."

"Watch your step. Here's the car."

After he had turned toward town, she said, "Was the college girl any help?"

"No. But she wasn't what I expected. I liked her. She made me feel a hundred and ten. She hasn't exactly found out what the world is all about, but her basic instincts are good, and they're slowly swinging her around like a compass that has to point the right way eventually. But she's fighting it every inch of the way. She kept trying to shock me. And that would be a pretty good trick. Kids her age, I've seen them brought in so rotted away with drugs, so diseased, so sexually abused they're in a semi-catatonic state. That's one part of cop work I don't miss."

"Well . . . I scored a big zero too. As a conspirator, Paul, I'm worse than useless."

She had not finished by the time they reached the motel office. She went in and he waited until she came out with a key. She came to the car window and said, "I can walk this far at least. Suppose you put the car back by your place and kill about ten minutes and then come and hear the rest of it."

She opened the door as soon as he knocked. She wore a yellow quilted robe. Her face was scrubbed and shiny, and she had made a white turban of one of the motel towels. It struck him that it gave the modeling of her face a cleaner look, and perhaps her normal hair styling was not as becoming as a more severe style would be.

When they were seated she made a rueful face and said, "One in the morning. Maybe listening to confessions is beyond the call of duty. Bill me for overtime, Paul. Where was I? Oh. Kelsey dragged me through what seemed like several miles of black wet woods, and I just came blundering along like a zombie, soaked to the skin. Then he trundled me up those stairs and into that place of his and pushed me into a chair. He made two stiff drinks and put one in my hand. Believe me, I pretended to drink it. He sat on the bed and worked on his and kept up this eerie monologue. I don't know how he got so terribly drunk so fast. But he seemed to really believe I was Lucille. And there was . . . a dangerousness about him. You know? I didn't want to make the slightest objection or cross him in any way. He hit that Mr. Furrbritt a terrible blow in the face. I don't know how badly he was hurt. Kelsey did a lot of rambling and mumbling, and there was a lot of it I couldn't follow. But he was trying to talk Lu into coming back to him. Everything would be different. And every once in a while he'd give me a horrible leer and tell me how happy he was going to make me when he took me to bed. I was sober by then, you can believe me. And I knew that if I could get out the door, I could outrun him. But he was closer to the door than I was. Right in the middle of a sentence he just toppled over onto his side and began to snore. When I was absolutely certain he was asleep, I phoned you. And waited and phoned again. And waited and phoned again. Then when you said you'd be right out, bless you, I crept out onto that porch and waited in the dark for you."

"But absolutely no results on the other thing?"

"Unless you count what George Furrbritt said about sacks of money and secret agreements and Sam Kimber having rough friends and so on." She frowned and shook her head slowly. "Oh, I have a lot of useful excuses. I was so emotionally exhausted I was vulnerable. And like a fool I gulped down that monstrous martini. And the storm and the lights going out made everything kind of unreal. And he really was a very skillful and mature and self-confident and reasonably attractive man. You know, when a man is the least bit tentative or apologetic or uncertain, it leaves you good places to say no. But when they just carry you along . . . oh, hell, Paul, I can give myself all the benefit of every doubt until hell freezes over, but I'm still going to be left with the crawly realization that while I was drifting along with it like a dreamy idiot, thinking about it as if it was some sort of sardonic game we were playing, that sleek son of a gun came within about three hot breaths of tipping me over behind the potted trees, and I have the horrible feeling that the instant I was jolted back to reality would have been the instant it was a little bit too late. It makes you think."

"But the lights did come back on, so you'll never know."

"Golly, I didn't come down here to indulge in any agonizing reappraisal of myself. I've sometimes felt wretched, and I've made some very bitter mistakes, but never before have I felt like a cheap, amiable floozie."

"Maybe there's something in the air out there."

She smiled at him. "You're quite nice. And now I'm feeling shy. I thought I was cold sober, but I wasn't. Suddenly I'm quite shocked at myself for the . . . intimate revelations. So maybe now I'm getting sober."

"There isn't anybody else to talk to."

"Of course. In a way, that makes it worse. The compulsive confessor."

"Not your fault, Barbara. It's a cop talent. I look understanding and nod at the right places and hang on every word and make little sympathetic sounds. People tell me everything."

"I bet they do at that, you poor guy. And you couldn't care less."

"Sometimes yes, sometimes no. And when I want to hear more, I can always drop the significant question in the right place."

"Let's hear one."

His eyes wavered momentarily. He moistened his lips. "Sure. Who was Roger?"

He saw her stiffen and saw her mouth change. He met her glance and he was the first to look away, but not before he sensed, from a change in his pulse, that their emotional relationship to each other had suddenly changed.

"You *are* very good at that, Paul."

"Cancel that one. It was a mistake."

She took a cigarette from the pack on the table. The angle of the lamp light made her smooth face, under the turban, as empty as a mask. In the V-neck of the robe her throat was a soft column, firm, with a dusky pocket at the base of it. He looked for a visible pulse and saw none, but knew that if he held his lips there he could feel a pulse against them. He experienced such a rush and torment of desire for her, he felt his shoulders lift, and felt the small creak of his back teeth as his jaw tightened. She was still looking down, gravely and thoughtfully. She shifted her quilted yellow hips in the chair. She gave such an aura of roundness, such a long slow firm roundness of arm and roundness of leg, dusky-sweet and tentative—a lip curling just so, an eyelid creased just so, and the soft clue to breasts set uncommonly wide in the long round torso. It was no longer possible for him to diminish his awareness of her by telling himself this was indeed quite a plain girl, solemn, rather sulky looking, too self-involved. Desire had worked too much of its transforming magic, and objectivity could not suppress the growing inventory of small delights and perfections.

She lifted her gaze suddenly, staring across at him through the slow gray lift of smoke, a gray-green stare, ancient and challenging.

"In that one letter, of course. But you see, you ask a good question and get a tiresome answer. He is a very decent man, really. A few years older than you, I'd say. With a look of sadness and patience. But he could make you laugh. A half-defeated man. Three children, and a wife with a totally dull and ordinary and inflexible mind. But very sincere and very dependent. There are always stages, you know. It started with liking. With friendship. Working in the same place all day, laughing at the same things. So you explore points of view, and find so much alike it turns into wistful romantic love, all very bittersweet and sad because you know you can't do anything about it. And the whole city turns into a sort of foreign film, so that even the way the birds fly has artistic significance. So with a terrible reluctance, inch by inch, you talk each other into thinking that somehow you have *earned* the right to go to bed. And that means plots of course, schemes and inner shiverings and a girlish terror of anticipation. And it is going to be magic, of course. Our little bit of happiness. Ah, we are such ineffably precious people, the little vulgarities of assignation will not touch us at all!"

"What are you trying to do to yourself?"

"It's been done, and it's over, Paul Stanial. We outgrew the sighings, the wine and candlelight phase very quickly. To our mutual astonishment, because we never thought of ourselves that way, it turned into an intensely physical affair. What was supposed to be just the affirmation of love, the symbol of love, became the end in itself, keeping us so drugged and so busy there was no time for love. And one day after a long time of it, too long a time of it, I went off to that dreary little room. He had to be late that day. There was one window. I stood at the window and looked at the people on the street, three stories below. There was a very cold pale winter light. I was so anxious for him it made me feel sick. There was a bar across the street. I saw a man and a woman come out. They were not young. They stood and seemed to be arguing. Suddenly he grabbed the front of her coat and began to beat her, cuffing her face forehand and backhand with deliberate blows that knocked her head halfway around each time. And I thought, in my superiority, how vulgar, how tawdry and crude and shameful. He released her and the woman went crying up the street, her shoulders all huddled. He stood with his fists on his hips and watched her go, and then he spat into the street and went back into the bar. I turned from the window and saw how the little room looked in that cold light. It was not a room in any loving or living sense. It was just a bed with walls around it. We'd

stopped having very much to say to each other. Suddenly I
realized it took an effort for me to see his face with any
clarity. And there were thousands and thousands of people like this in little rooms like this, emptying themselves of
their horrid little itchings, forgetting each other's face and
having very little to say. It was a vulgarity worse than being
beaten in the street. It couldn't possibly be me in that room. It
was like waking up in a hospital with no memory of the accident. I put my clothes back on as fast as I could and got out
of there, because I knew that if he arrived before I left, I
might never have the will to leave again. The next day, the
day I quit my job, I had coffee with him in a crowded place.
And there still wasn't anything to say, very much. Just sort of
good-by. I told Lu about it, eventually. I think she tried to understand. But she looked at me strangely—as if she'd heard
I was a thief. Or took drugs. My resignation didn't go
through. He got me transferred to a different office in the
same firm."

She looked at him with a half-smile and a quizzical frown.
"I thought I was so unique. And any situation I got into
would be special because it was me. But I got into one of
the most ordinary tiresome situations in the world. The office affair. Everything we said to each other from the beginning, if there was a tape of it, and tapes of a hundred other
couples, I'll bet the only way you could tell them apart is by
the names. All the rest of it is alike." Her eyes filled and the
tears broke loose, ran slowly down, effecting no change in
her expression.

"You listen so *well*," she said, and wiped her eyes on the
yellow sleeve.

"Who are you making fun of now?"

"Both of us, Paul. Both of us."

"Can you sleep now?"

"How did you know I wouldn't have been able to, until
now?"

"You seemed tense. Now you don't." He stood up. After
he had opened the door onto the warm night, he turned in
the doorway and took hold of her arms just above the elbows. He sensed her uncertainty, her vulnerability, her subdued alarm. He could sense exactly what she was thinking.

He gave her a little shake, a small gruffness of affection.
"Sleep well," he said and walked into the night. He heard
the door close. He walked slowly to his own place, feeling a
smugness of great virtue and restraint. He knew he could

have taken her. The day had cast her adrift, and she was there for the taking. Salvage, to be towed to the closest port. But, as salvage, a motorless, rudderless craft. It would all be on his terms, not hers. Sleep and time would restore her.

After he was in bed it occurred to him there might never be another chance. His smugness evaporated. If that was the way it turned out, he had made the wrong choice of regrets. Which, too, was part of the pattern which dogged him. The vast vault of the silky night stretched over ten times ten thousand tousled, dreaming, round-legged girls, gentle and humid and golden in the night silence, their breathing sweet, their pillowed hair soft and long, and on the cruel bachelor rack he loved every one and wanted every one, without names, without tensions, without regrets—just a long sweet worship at the shrine of girlness in the tangly night.

# Ten

SHERIFF HARV WALMO stood on the weedy sidewalk of Tyler Street and looked at Paul Stanial with an expression of mournful irritation. "Damn it to hell, I can't go by the way you *feel* about it."

"I just said it seems a little too neat."

"All I can go by are the facts turned up in my investigation. He left his office about quarter to twelve. It looks like he figured on going back there on account of the way he left stuff spread all over his desk. They say he always picked up. Maybe his heart was starting to go and it felt stuffy to him in the office so he drove around for air. I know Sam Kimber fired him yesterday and flang him out of the office bodily. So he was driving around, maybe feeling worse, and when it hit him he didn't even get a chance to stop the car. But his foot was off the gas so it was moving slow. You can see where it bunked the curb over there and then came on over across here, and you can see the track it made right on over to that cabbage palm it hit dead on, but not hard. Then that Mrs. Antry, she phoned in about looking out her bedroom window and seeing a car in the lot with the lights on and the motor running, and my deputy checked and radioed in for the ambulance. But he was past needing an ambulance. What the hell, Stanial, the man had a rough day losing a big account and he was working hard. Besides, the coroner *says* it was a heart attack."

"I'm sorry, Sheriff. I just say it seems too neat. What was he doing over here?"

"Just riding around I'd say. This isn't any kind of through street to anyplace. Just riding around in the night."

"He's tied into the Lucille Hanson thing."

"How? What does that mean? Because he's worked for Sam Kimber a long time? Stanial, I said it before and I'll say it again. You got anything looks like legal evidence, you can bring it to me and I'll open it all up. I haven't got a closed mind on this thing. But I just can't go ahead with nothing to go on. You got the first thing you can give me?"

"Not yet."

"Then if you'll excuse me, I got to go back to my office where there's a lot of other things with something to go on. I suppose you fellas like to stretch these here things out as long as you can."

"Not this time, Sheriff. Thanks for the personal tour."


Mrs. Betty Schaud, Gus Gable's secretary, was a small spare woman with iron-gray hair, a cold square face, and all the social charm of the attendant in a gas chamber. It was only with the greatest reluctance she let Paul Stanial use the telephone. He phoned upstairs to Sam Kimber and stated his problem. Kimber told him to put the Schaud woman on. He handed her the phone. He could hear the measured and emphatic resonance of Sam Kimber's voice. The woman did not change expression, but her face became sweaty, and red spots of color appeared in her cheeks.

After she hung up she said, "This is all very unusual."

"Sudden death is always a little bit unusual."

"Come this way."

She took him into Gus' private office. The big desk was piled with folders and stacks of documents. "The Sheriff examined this room," she said. "As soon as our Mr. Grady has a chance, he'll go over this work and dispose of it properly. Please understand that this is a special favor to Mr. Kimber. I wouldn't say you have any legal right to be here. Whatever you want, please do it. I have other work to do." She stood beside the desk and folded starched arms.

When Stanial sat in Gable's chair, she gave a snort of disapproval. He looked at the documents on the desk. They all seemed to refer to some aspect of Kimber's varied operations.

The desk pad was a big scratch pad, the top sheet covered with a maze of doodles and numerals. The switch-button telephone was on a side table. There was a smaller scratch pad beside it. He rolled the chair closer and examined the top sheet. After some silent minutes of examination, he stood up and tore the top sheet off.

"Not one scrap of paper leaves this office," Mrs. Schaud said.

He handed it to her. She looked at it and then looked at him, puzzled. "This is just doodling. But I can't let you have it anyway."

"Got a Verifax or equivalent? I'd like a copy. Keep the original in a safe place."

She gave the sigh of someone imposed upon to the limit of endurance. He waited in the outer office. She disappeared and reappeared with a clear copy. He took it up to Sam Kimber's office. Angie Powell looked crisp and lively in a blue and white striped blouse and a blue skirt. He guessed that she saved that particularly vivid smile of welcome for people who had gained Mister Sam's approval.

He went into Kimber's office and closed the door.

"How are things down there?"

"Running on momentum, I guess."

"What I'll do, I'll leave it up to that Bruner and McCabe to get my records out of there. All morning I've geen wondering if what I did helped kill that little son of a bitch. What have you got there?"

Stanial explained what it was. He went around behind the desk and studied it over Kimber's shoulder.

"What the hell does it mean?"

"Maybe nothing. Maybe it's stuff he wrote down last week. But there's this twelve in block letters, underlined, and he left the office at quarter of."

"So it could have been an appointment he made over the phone?"

"And if so, this other stuff might be a clue to the appointment."

Kimber touched the crude drawing of a buxom female torso with a fingertip. "With a woman, if this means anything. But what the hell is this f-r-n-t-r?"

"I don't know, but look over here. Tyler. That's why I got interested in this thing. That's where he died. Tyler Street."

"But that's got initials. A. P. Tyler. It doesn't have to mean the street. This funny thing, this f-r-n-t-r, it looks as if it has smoke coming off of it, Paul."

"I can't figure out what . . ."

"Wait a minute! There was a furniture store on Tyler that burned about a year ago. Hell, Stanial, are we getting too carried away on this thing? It's so mixed up you can invent about anything you want."

"So let's go take a look at it."

Kimber hesitated, shrugged. "Why not?"

Sam Kimber was the one to spot the cigar near the base of the pile of covered lumber. He picked it up, rolled it between his fingers. "Dry," he said. "So it wasn't out here in the rain. Don't know if it's Gus' brand. See the wrapper anyplace?" Stanial found it by a tuft of grass. Kimber identified it as Gus' customary brand. Stanial investigated the area with painstaking care. He found another cigar butt, as dry as the unlighted one. He found enough fragments of ash which the hard rain would have washed away to indicate Gus had spent some time in the area.

"Where is this getting us?" Sam demanded.

"A suppositional structure. He had a midnight date here. He could have sat on this lumber and waited. Maybe the other party showed up, maybe not. He peeled this cigar and bit the end off, but he never lit it. Why? Maybe suddenly he felt sick and dropped it and barely managed to get to his car and get it started before he died. Or maybe the other party started a scuffle. Maybe the exertion killed him, and they stuck him in the car and got him rolling. Too bad these damn cinders won't take a track."

"Not very much, is it?"

"Not enough to go to Walmo with. Maybe enough to take to the lab section of a big metropolitan force and have them vacuum this area down to the last blade of grass. But not enough for Walmo."

They made slow progress back out to the curb, with Stanial looking carefully for any further sign or track.

Kimber leaned against his car, his expression sour. "You know what we're both thinking, don't you? I never got a chance to get back to Gus, and maybe if I did, I could have shook a little more information out of him. And maybe somebody realized it."

"The next step is an autopsy, if Walmo can be hustled into it."

"I can hustle him," Kimber said grimly.

He walked around the car to get in, and stopped suddenly. "What's the matter?"

"Come here." Mystified, Stanial followed him across the street and about a hundred feet south. He stopped near the school and pointed beyond the school building. "See through there? That gray house? You can't see much of it. The Powell house. Angie. Angie Powell. A. P. And that girl drawing." He looked at Stanial with a strained expression. "And now you've got me doing it, because that's plain going too damn far."

"Are you sure?"

"Listen, I know Angie as well as I . . ."

"You told her you thought Gus might try to make trouble for you."

"And she looked worried on account of she is loyal. That's all. Chrissake, Paul, if she went around knocking off everybody who . . ."

"There's something strange about her. You know she didn't approve of Lucille."

"Strange? She's just a very decent, religious, clean-living girl is all."

"Then why do you have to shout that at me, Sam?"

Kimber took out a handkerchief and mopped his face. "I just know we're on the wrong track. That's all."

"But she's in a position to know a great deal about your personal affairs and habits, Sam. She could know about the money."

"I don't see how."

"From Gus?"

"God, Stanial, I don't know."

"She's a big powerful young girl."

"Everybody likes Angie."

"And she's like a fish in the water, apparently."

"Why would she want that money?"

"Would it be the money? I don't know. I talked to her the day I was trying to see you for the first time. She sounded odd. I can't put my finger on it. She sounded emotionally disturbed."

Kimber wiped his face again. "Take all that walking back and forth through the office and it gets you to thinking. Lot of girl. A big ol' back-buster of a girl, so one time I made my try. Before Lucille come along. The look in her eyes, it would like to make you cry. Told me she promised God and her mother she'd never do anything dirty. Thought she had to quit right then and there. Paul, I just don't know. It doesn't seem possible."

"I think I know the next step. If we are guessing right, we should know a lot more than she thinks we know. In police work, that's always a position of strength. The person you are talking to can't decide what to admit and what to deny. I think that by talking to her I can get a good idea of how wrong we are. Or how right. Can we catch her before she goes to lunch?"

"There's time," Sam said.

"Order her to go to lunch with me and order her to co-operate with me. Don't say what about."

They went back and got into the car. Sam Kimber shook his head. "Right now it's making me feel a little bit sick. But I know that soon as I walk into the office and see her there, I'm going to know we've just been talking each other into a mess of foolishment."

The hostess led them back to a table for two. Paul, following behind Angie, was aware of the attention she got from the men in the dining room. She was worth looking at, from the lively flex and bounce of the dark gold hair down to the round, even glide of golden legs below the edge of the blue skirt. The skirt swung with her walk and the hips were a swell of tautness under blue fabric, and her wide shoulders in the blue and white striped blouse tapered down across a flatness of back to her strong waist. "Hah you, Angie," they said. And, "Hi there, Angela honey." And, "Afternoon, Miss Powell." She waved and spoke and smiled. They gave him cool speculative glances.

He held the chair for her and then sat down facing her. Her eyes sparkled as she smiled at him. "Mostly lunch is a quick counter sandwich, Mr. Stanial, so this is a treat."

The waitress brought the water and said, "Sure beat us a close one last night, Angie."

"You did real good though, Clara. Golly, you sure are a dead-eye on those spares."

"If you can't get strikes, you got to do something. The corn beef is real good today."

"Okay for me. Clara, this is Mr. Stanial and he's a *in*surance man. Clara Wikely."

"How do," Clara said. "I had the corn beef myself and it sure is good."

"Two then," Paul said. "And coffee."

"Milk for me," Angie said. When the waitress left, she looked across at Stanial with less of a smile, and with a questioning candor in her lavender eyes.

"Mister Sam was sure mysterious about sending me on off with you, Mr. Stanial."

"Make it Paul."

"And you call me Angie, huh?"

"You bowled last night?"

"Up against Clara's team in the league last night, and we started bad but we got lucky. What is it you want to talk to me about, Paul?"

"I'm not really an insurance man, Angie."

"No?"

He leaned toward her. "I'm here to investigate the murder of Lucille Hanson."

"The *what*?" She looked genuinely shocked. "Oh, come now, Paul! If that was a murder, why everybody would be talking about it all day long."

"Why couldn't it be?"

"Well . . . I suppose it *could* be. But there wouldn't be hardly anything to go on. I mean if it *was* a murder, there wouldn't hardly be much sense to it, would there? Are you kidding me or something?"

"I'm completely and totally serious. And I'd hoped to get some very useful information from Gus Gable. As a matter of fact, I talked to him on the phone last night about it."

To his annoyance, the waitress arrived with the lunch at that moment and in the distraction he was unable to tell if he had scored. She took a hungry mouthful and looked at him and said, "Now what would Gus know about anything like that?"

"Angie, I didn't bring you to lunch to ask you what you think Gus might have known about the murder of Lucille Hanson."

"Gee, it sounds funny to hear you say murder. What do you want to ask me?"

"What you talked to Gus about last night."

If the fork hesitated on its way to the healthy mouth, it was a faltering so minor he was unable to detect it. But she looked considerably less friendly.

"What gives you the idea I talked to Gus last night?"

"He said he was going to see you."

She did not look alarmed. She looked thoughtful and annoyed. She said, "I sure didn't see him."

"Then why did he say that?"

"You know, I don't know as it's any of your business. Let me think a minute." She ate steadily and efficiently. She cleaned her plate and pushed it an inch or so away and put her elbows on the table and looked at him. "I had planned on telling this to Mister Sam sooner or later, so I might as well tell you now, seeing as how you could be getting the wrong idea. You're an investigator and I suppose you can check it all out. Last night while I was bowling a call came for me and I couldn't take it then, and I wasn't in any hurry to call back. It was from Gus and I recognized his office number. I had a pretty good idea why he was calling. Well, after bowling I went to Ernie's with some of the girls on the team and had something to eat, and when they left, I went to the phone there and called Gus. He was awful upset. Losing Sam's account meant a lot to him, and like I thought, he had the idea I could help him get it back. He wanted to see me. He had some ideas he wanted to talk over with me. I told him I didn't want to be seen anywhere with somebody Mister Sam threw out. He was almost in tears. He hinted he'd make it worth my while. He begged and pleaded, but honest, I just didn't want to see him. So he said he'd drive over at midnight and park near that burned furniture place, handy to my house where nobody could see us, and we'd talk it over and I'd never be sorry. I still said no. Now I don't know whether he went there or not, and I don't know as I care much. But seeing he had his attack right there on Tyler, maybe he did, hoping I'd change my mind. And if he said he was going to see me, he was just wishing out loud. I went right home from Ernie's and I talked to my mother for a little while and then we went to bed and I didn't go out. You can ask my folks. The siren woke me up as I was going to sleep, but I didn't have any way of knowing it was on account of Gus dying right near my house."

There she was, looking at him with the right amount of indignation and righteousness on her big bland All-American girl face, with the little smile lines bracketing the muscular curvature of her lips, with two tiny chickenpox craters on the bland expanse of brow, and a little sun-white fuzz on her upper lip, with some whitened squint-lines at the outside corners of her eyes, a crumb of roll-crust on her solid chin.

He could see past the wiry roots of her hair to the white meat of her scalp. Her sleeveless blouse exposed the smooth and rounded slabs of muscle that slid under the useful hide as she moved her arms. Earnest in the irises of lavender were the little black orifices of pupil, oiled with health, letting his own image through to the invisible rods and cones. She was a wide-screen projection of a girl, and he felt an abrupt shift of awareness in his mind, and he wondered what the hell he was doing here and what he was talking about. Here, as Sam Kimber understood, was the acme of plausibility. The money would turn up. Lucille had hid it a little too well after Gus made her nervous. Lucille had cramped and gasped and lost her composure and drowned. And Gus had looked like a heart case. Here was glowing plausibility, and also a sadness—the same kind of regretful sadness as when you see any superb mechanism used for a lesser purpose than its designer intended. This was a big, remarkable, almost terrifying engine of a girl, with enough warmth and energy to spawn and raise a dozen kids, and enough left over to keep a durable husband faithful. But some little sprocket had been bent, and the chain had slipped, and the machine was useful as a secretary or a bowling partner or an opponent in a foot race. Here, he suspected, the unwanted juices would dry early, and in another fifteen years she would be a leathery parody of woman. But now she reminded him of a bowl of artificial fruit.

But he had to continue the cop reflex, and take the test the rest of the way, though his heart was not in it.

"Angie, I guess you've explained almost everything."

"I'm not explaining anything. I'm just telling you."

"Then if you're just telling me, then tell me what you were doing walking through that school yard last night after midnight."

She shook her head almost sadly. "I swear, Paul, you must be trying some kind of silly trick, and I don't know what you're trying to get at. If anybody says they saw me, they're out of their mind. Or lying."

He sighed. "Okay, Angie. No more questions."

"It's a crazy thing anyhow, thinking Miz Hanson was murdered. I suppose you think Gus was murdered too?" She looked startled and then her eyes narrowed. "If you *do* think he was murdered too, then you must be thinking I did it."

"It crossed my mind."

"You got a sick mind, Mister Stanial. I swear. I should be

mad at you, but it makes me want to laugh somehow. Golly!
Wondering if I killed both of them. Honest, I just don't have
that much free time. And I live by the commandments, Paul.
Thou shalt not kill. Does anybody else have such a crazy
idea. Hey, did it cross Mister Sam's mind too?"

"He tried to believe it might be possible, but he just
couldn't."

"It's that he knows me better than that. No harm done,
I guess. It's all just . . . sort of silly."

She seemed so absolutely normal he felt an idle urge to
make her disclose that other part of herself, that sing-song
glaze of the practicing fanatic. "Sam will be himself again
as soon as he ties up with another woman," he said casually.
"You think so much of him, maybe you ought to give him
his comfort closer to home. You're a big healthy girl and
there's no boyfriend to object, is there?"

It interested him to watch her face change. The mouth
narrowed and the firm cheeks seemed to flatten, and he could
see the whites of her eyes all around the iris. "I would crawl
through fiery coals for Mister Sam. But I'd not add more
damage to his immortal soul by offering my flesh to him in
sin. And I don't like this kind of dirty talk."

"Do you really think Sam's relationship with Lucille Hanson
damaged either of them?"

"Her more than him, if there was anything left to be
damaged. She was a lustful whore that enticed him, and the
fires of hell were waiting to consume her evil body and
she'll roast down there for eternity."

"Oh come now, Angie! Isn't that just fright talking? Who
scared you so badly? Your mother? How do you expect to
lead a normal life."

"I wasn't put here to lead a normal life."

He was suddenly alert. "What were you put here for?"

"To . . . to be an example."

"Well, the example isn't changing the ways of the world
much."

"This is the time of sin. God has turned His back."

"On you too?"

"There's some gifted to see His face."

"That makes you a very special person, doesn't it?"

She blushed and looked down. "Taking pride in it would
be a sin."

"Does He tell you what to do?"

The blush faded and she sat very still for too long a time.

She raised her lids and looked across the table at him. "Maybe one day He will speak to me. I pray for that day."

"Didn't God make man and woman with some functional idea in mind?"

She looked at him with what he thought was a strange intensity. "Do you think you could change the way I feel about the sins of the flesh?"

"Let's say I think your attitude leaves something to be desired, Angie."

"And you'd like to be the one to help me? And maybe take me back to Miami with you? Have you seduced other virgins with your sweet talk and your blue eyes, Mister Stanial?"

"Now wait a minute."

"You didn't care about their immortal souls. You said your sly little love words, and then you desecrated them, and God will not forgive you. You're black with sin, Mister Stanial."

"Actually I think I'm quite a decent guy."

She seemed to give a little shake, a little flexure of muscles, and changed back into the person she was before. "I think you're nice enough, Paul, honest. It's just that when two people don't think the same way, I guess they shouldn't talk about religion." She smiled appealingly. "I'm not going to change you and you're not going to change me. But just please don't ever talk dirty in front of me like you did. It makes me feel crawly."

"Okay, Angie."

"Where'd Clara get to? I got to be getting back."

As she turned to look for the waitress, the light caught the underside of her right forearm, and he saw the pattern of small puckered white scars.

"What happened to your arm?"

She turned back. "What?"

He reached and took her wrist and turned her arm. "These marks?"

Her hand was yanked away with shocking force, and he felt his face go blank with astonishment as he looked into the third face of Angie Powell, saw the lips lifted up and back from the strong white teeth, the eyes bright slits, heavy cords stretching the smooth skin of her throat.

"Don't ever touch me," she whispered, and he sensed it took her a special effort to form each word, as though it was a language she did not speak well.

And then he saw her walking away quite briskly between

the tables, silhouetted against the bright front windows of the restaurant.

He phoned Sam from the restaurant phone before paying his check.

"Well?" Sam said.

"After the first fifteen minutes, I was on your side. Now I don't know."

"And what the hell does that mean?"

"It means a psychotic doesn't play the game according to the rules. She's on her way back now. What are those scars on her arm?"

"Those little white marks? Like a lot of vaccinations. I don't know. I asked her once, and she got sort of upset so I didn't push it."

"I don't know why she's so sensitive about them. Sam, even if she checks out clean, that girl needs help."

"Doc Nile told me that once, too. But what the hell am I supposed to do? She does her work. She gets along with everybody. She's just now coming in."

"Sam, how does she . . ."

"Hold it a minute."

After two minutes Sam came back on the line. In a low voice he said, "Cheery as a clam. Said she had a nice lunch. Said it came as a shock to her about you and me having to find out who she'd killed lately. It's a joke to her, Paul. Now, dammit, get her off your mind and find out who really did kill my girl."


Ernie said, "Sure, I remember Angie making a call. After she walked out with the other gals, she come back in and made a call and she was in the booth there quite a spell. Then we talked some and she took off. . . . You're quite welcome, mister. No trouble at all. Only what's it about?"


The stooped, lethargic, hollow-eyed man at Happy Lanes said, "Call for Angie? Not over this phone, not last night, mister. Nobody gets back of this here counter but me, and nobody touches this phone, so come the end of the month I don't get any long-distance bills I don't remember. It could have come on the pay phone over in the restaurant part, but if a person was calling here, it would come on this phone just about always because it's the one in the book."

The front hall of the little gray house smelled musty, and Angie's monstrous mother had a voice like a prolonged screech. She loomed like an enraged hippo in the shadowy sultry air. "She was home some after eleven and she didn't go out again, and I demand to know what kind of questions you think you're asking and what right you got asking them. I raised me a decent clean girl and we got no secrets between us, and the last thing in the world she'd be doing would be sneaking out. Oh, I know all about the other young girls in this town, how they go scampering off in the brush every chance they get, rolling onto their backs for anything wears pants, but my Angela ain't one of them."

"This is just a routine insurance investigation."

"I bet it is. I just bet it is. Routine, hah? Making yourself a chance to bring Angie in on something she's got nothing to do with so you can come snuffling around after her. You just might as well give up, mister, because you nor nobody else is going to get anyplace with my Angie. I taught her early and I taught her good. No man alive is going to lay his stinking hands on her sweet body. Men got just that one thing on their mind, day and night, and the good Lord knows there's enough sluts in this town you can find to pleasure you just by snapping your fingers, so you don't have to come around here."

"I'm afraid you have the wrong idea, Mrs. Powell."

She tilted ponderously toward him, a sneer imbedded in the pouches of fat. "You know something, young man? I have wrong ideas *all* the time. I walk out into the world and I look on every side, and my mind reels with the number of wrong ideas I have." She pointed a finger like a small uncooked pork sausage at the center of his face. "And every single one of them turns out to be right. So you get on out of my house."

After he had stepped out, he turned back and spoke to the shadowy vastness through the screen. "By the way, how did she get those scars on her arm?"

"Mortifying the flesh, mister. Mortifying the flesh to drive out the devil, which is something you wouldn't understand."

It took Doctor Rufus Nile ten minutes each for the last three patients, while Stanial waited. Nile had a yen for some cold beer, so he locked the office and they drove to a dark, cool, pleasant, downtown tavern where they carried the large steins of dark draught beer back to a paneled booth with a scarred, scrubbed table-top.

"When a man doesn't take the first opening he gets, it means he has a small speech planned," Nile said. He thrust his chin toward Paul and boggled his eyes. "Hah?"

"A careful statement, because it might be tied in with professional ethics. In my investigation of whether or not it was an accidental drowning or suicide, I seem to have opened up another possibility, Doctor. And it could involve somebody you seem to have had a professional opinion about. So I'll be blunt about it. Do you think Angie Powell is capable of murder?"

Nile gave several little jumps of surprise and consternation. He smacked his lips, tugged his ear, patted his chest, turned his stein around and around.

"Let me get organized here. Hah? First off, psychiatry isn't my field. Second, Angie was the second delivery I made after I took over the practice in this place. Third, I like Angie. I think I understand her from knowing something of the background. Murder? That would be a pretty drastic way of expressing some disapproval, wouldn't it?"

"On any logical basis. But is she logical?"

"Mary Powell was a bad patient. Seems like the minute she found out she was pregnant she started stuffing herself. Just three months married when she got pregnant. Acted as if she'd caught leprosy from little Jimmy. Treated Jimmy for some prostate trouble a few years back, and I know for a fact that from the day she found out she was pregnant, she never let Jimmy resume marital relations with her. Frankly, she hated it so much I could say stuffing herself was a defense against it, but I'm no psychiatrist. The forty pounds she put on while she was carrying Angie made it a difficult birth. But it was a fine healthy girl baby. And Mary kept right on eating. And the bigger she got the more religious she got. Must be three hundred pounds now, and got just about the meanest temper in town."

"And Angie got her sexual orientation from her mother?"

"Give you an example. Angie was a sunny little girl, popular with the other kids. Anyway, there was a little boy in the neighborhood. Can't recall his name. They moved away long ago. Angie was about seven years old, I'd judge. Children have sexual curiosity. Absolutely normal all over the world. In primitive tribes, who are more enlightened about these things than we are, it is accepted. But if we catch the kids, we try to convince them they've done something filthy. Same as our cultural attitude toward masturbation. We try to make out only sick kids do it, and we try to pretend it isn't a perfectly normal and natural stage in sexual development of the individual, that is only a mild clinical symptom of immaturity if it continues into the adult years.

"So one afternoon Mary Powell just happens to go around the garage and there is Angie and the neighbor boy solemnly examining each other. She moves fast for a big woman. She give the boy a crack across the face that sends him howling home with two broken teeth, and she yanks up a stake out of the garden and she beats her daughter as bad as I've ever heard of a kid being beaten without killing it. Mary should have been jailed and damned near was, and would have been if the church hadn't gotten behind her. Angie was three weeks in the hospital. Broken ribs, ruptured kidney, contusions, abrasions, lacerations, internal bleeding. She was my case, and I guess it was the last time any male creature has seen Angie in her birthday suit. For female problems, she and her mother go to a lady doctor in Orlando. Time she got released, she was a little hollow-eyed ghost, and just about as quiet as one. Mary kept her out of school all that year. And she was one silent little girl for at least two years after that. Anybody could guess that with a background like that, that girl was going to have some trouble in her adolescence. And she did, when she was fifteen. They brought her to me from the high school with a high fever and a badly infected arm. It could have killed anybody less husky. I slapped her into the hospital and for the first twenty-four hours, I wasn't sure. The infection started with a burn. And there were other burns on the underside of that same arm, some of them healed and some of them still scabbed. And I could not find out how she got them. Not until I stuck a little sodium pentothal into her, and suddenly I had a classic case of hysteria on my hands. Complete muscular rigidity, marble pallor, gibberish about dreams and visions, and some crazy identification with Joan of Arc. The fool child was holding her arm in a candle flame, and from the marks she'd done it about fifteen times."

"And endure pain like that!"

"A good galloping case of hysteria with religious overtones has elements of auto-hypnosis in it, and there's a good chance she couldn't even feel the pain. Like the optimistic idiot I am, I talked to Mary about getting help for the girl. But Mary was proud of her! Imagine that?"

"Mortification of the flesh. Driving out the devil."

Nile stared at him keenly. "Her words exactly. I guess you can understand the burning. Here was a girl . . . is a girl . . . with superb physical equipment. All the glands are working. She ovulates and she's got big useful breasts and a good fertile pelvic structure, and the female hormones are feeding into her system right on schedule. Now if she could have yearned for the normal sexual experience, but avoided it because she thought it was wrong, then she would have been left with just a feeling of guilt and shame for having such evil instincts. But here is a big healthy girl so emotionally crippled there's no yearning at all, no curiosity, no feeling of guilt. It was pounded into her with a garden stake long ago that any sex thought is horrifying and nauseating. So, emotionally, it does nauseate her. And there is that fine body with no outlet. Hence the hysteria. The religious visions. The whole sickening ball of wax. Mary Powell ought to be fed to the 'gators for doing that to her own child."

"Can that inner conflict make her dangerous?"

"Back to murder? Hah? It could. Under the right circumstances, it could. But it wouldn't be murder to her. She wouldn't do anything she thought was wrong."

"It would be execution?"

"Exactly."

"Which would exempt her from the legal definition of sanity, the knowledge of right and wrong. Tell me, Doctor, could she think God instructed her to kill?"

"God, or Joan of Arc, or Father Divine. It's the classic rationalization. She would think of herself as an instrument, obedient to outside orders."

"Could such murders be cleverly done under those circumstances?"

"I've heard they can be. And the murderer has one advantage over the normal kind."

"What's that?"

"They are absolutely sure of themselves, and so they don't get trapped by their own feeling of guilt. Stanial, I hope to God you're wrong. And I notice you said murders. Would you be thinking of Gus Gable?"

"Yes."

"Back in the office I've got an EKG on him three months old. Shows a healthy heart. Harv Walmo phoned me about that. So I guess by now Bert Dell has taken a look in there."

"Where would he do it?"

"Probably over to Crocker and Gain's place, because they didn't bother taking Gus to the hospital."

"Could you find out?"

Nile stood up and selected a dime from his change. "Bert loves to do autopsies, and he loves to talk about them."

Nile was frowning when he came back to the table five minutes later, carrying two fresh steins. He sat down and said, "Not a hell of a lot of sense to it. Bruised and ruptured diaphragm. And the pericardium was ripped open and it looked to him as if the heart had been bruised somehow. With a congenital defect the pericardium can bust if you build up enough fluid pressure, but he couldn't see any signs of anything like that. That pericardium is thin, tough, elastic tissue. And the bruise was along the bottom sector of the right ventricle. Bert said a funny thing. He said it was like Gus had fallen just exactly right onto something blunt, like a fence post."

"Could it be done with a fist?"

Nile shook his head. "She's a big girl but she couldn't hit that hard. No man could either. Gus would have had to be in a slumped over position. Maybe some projecting object inside the car when it hit the tree."

"If that came second, why did he hit the tree?"

"And he didn't hit it hard, did he?"

"Doctor, you told Sam Kimber Angie needed help."

Nile nodded abruptly several times. He combed his wild hair with his fingers and huffed on the lenses of his glasses. "Last year she worked for me, part time. Came in Saturdays to get the billing straightened out. The girl who was doing the billing left in a hurry. She clipped about two thousand dollars from me, according to the auditors, and left. I had a feeling about Angie. She was . . . well, she was too perfect. Smiling and fast and efficient. Always the same. As if you could lift her blouse in the back and find the place for the key to wind her up. Sometimes that kind of . . . imperviousness is a clue to extreme tension."

"Doctor, did she have a key to your office?"

"Did she? Yes. She'd come in alone. Why?"

"Never mind. What were you saying?"

"I meddle. It's my curse. I wanted to see how much adjustment she'd made. I had a clinical photograph, eight by ten, an adult male. Fine specimen. I put it with some papers

I gave her. She came in and handed it back, saying it must have gotten in the papers by accident. She was as casual as a nurse. I didn't take it. I asked her what it was. She glanced at it again. She said it was a picture of a man in flowing white robes. She wasn't lying, Stanial. That was what she *saw*. Next time I saw Sam I told him she was a sick girl. No point in trying to tell her mother."

"Does she know anatomy?"

"Some. She trained to be a nurse but she dropped out after a few months. Oh, you mean about Gus? In the back of my mind I've been wondering. Could I cause that damage? How? Physically he was in very sloppy condition. I could put him out, brace him in a flexed position, and possibly, just possibly, if I didn't care if I tore him up a little, I could depress the diaphragm deeply enough to press my hand against the heart itself, stop it perhaps."

"She's a strong girl."

"She's not a monster, you know."

"But she could do a monstrous thing if she thought she had been told to do it. If she heard the right voices. And there's a sort of symbolism to it. It has the mark of insanity."

"If it was done that way!"

"What would make her talk about it?"

Nile shrugged. "Sodium pentothal again. Hypnosis. I'd say she's a good hypnotic subject. But it has to be at her request or at the request of the court, my friend. Hah?"

"I feel sorry for her, Doctor."

"She's an extreme case, certainly. But spare a little sorrow for the rest of them. More people than you could count have bitched up lives on account of this crazy culture. The Puritan heritage says that sex is nasty. Life says sex is constructive fun. So we go around smirking, sneaking, making it a nasty mystery. The most sex-conscious, sex-oppressed nation in history. I treat a lot of the by-products—frigidity, impotence, despair. And it's the most tortured ones, the most disturbed ones, who want to scrub what they think is filth out of their own minds, but they can't, so they want to censor everything they can reach because it makes them feel cleaner, and very righteous. Such a stinking fuss over the simple beautiful mechanics of fertilization. If clothes were against the law, we'd be cured in one generation. Hah?"

Nile dropped him off back at his car, and at the motel desk he found a note from Barbara saying she was at the motel pool. There was heft and dazzle in the late afternoon sun, but the high pile of thunderheads across the eastern sky gave the day an odd light. There were small gusts of hot wind which rattled the palm fronds. All the metal chairs under the faded umbrellas were empty, and she was alone in the small pool, in a white cap and a yellow suit, gliding with slow efficiency back and forth the length of the pool, shoulders rolling slightly, hands slipping into the water cleanly. From time to time one foot would lift too high, and the hard chunking sound revealed the power of her stroke. She did not see him until he walked around to the end and waited there for her. Then she stopped and clung to the gutter, slightly winded, and smiled up at him, squinting in the light, shaking the water out of her eyes.

"You're pretty good," he said.

"Out of condition. But I wanted to do something exhausting." She levered herself up into a sitting position on the apron and got to her feet. "And I saw a special on swim suits down the street. Three ninety-five." She walked ahead of him to the table where she had left her towel and sandals, walking with the constrained and slightly knock-kneed stride of the woman who knows herself observed. She yanked the cap off and fluffed her brown hair. There was a pink cast of fresh sunburn over the ivoried smoothness of her round arms and legs.

She dried her face and her bare shoulders and sat in the umbrella shade and looked up at him ruefully. "I talked an awful lot last night, Paul."

He moved the other chair into the shade and sat near her. "No need to feel apologetic."

"Not apologetic, exactly. Just sort of stupid and whiney."

"It was a bad day for you."

"Thank you for listening. And I want to stop feeling awkward with you. But I don't know how, exactly. Too much self-exposure went on."

He smiled at her. "How much is too much? Would you feel better if I tried to even it up? I can make some juicy confessions."

"Paul, I didn't mean . . ."

"Take last night. The attraction is strong. Don't tell me you haven't sensed it. And you were on the ragged edge of a sort of emotional collapse. And I came close to giving you another problem, and I don't think you could have coped."

"I . . . I don't know." She bit her lip. "But you didn't."

"No. I didn't. And after I got back to my place, I regretted it bitterly. What the hell, I said to myself. What are you trying to prove, Stanial? There it was and you walked away from it, and it won't ever be that easy again."

"But I don't . . ."

"I am not a very nice guy, Barbara. Maybe what I am trying to do right now, instead of making you feel better, is trying to set you up. And that's all I would want. No emotional obligations. No moral obligations. Just the simplest, oldest hunger in the world. Tip my hat and walk away. Thank you, m'am."

She looked at him with an oddly anguished expression, and in a barely audible voice said, "Maybe I'm not . . . worth any more than that."

"You're worth so much more . . . I walked away."

She dropped her glance, and her posture in the chair had a look of meekness, almost of supplication. In the curious orange sunlight the droplets of water from the pool glistened on the fine-grained texture of her knees and thighs.

"I'm not very valuable," she said.

"Don't be such a fool!" he said irritably.

She looked at him calmly and nodded, as though approving some inner statement. "Attraction, yes. I did sense that. And it doesn't mean much, I suppose. But I guess it's the only starting place people have. It flatters me, Paul. It's nice to have you want me. I guess I need that kind of reassurance these days. I've felt like a drab for a long time. I haven't liked myself very much."

"I like you."

"Which is just what I wanted to hear. And I like you, too. And that should be enough, I suppose. So I want to say okay. Let's. What difference would it possibly make to anybody in the world? But I can't be so . . . cold-blooded."

"I don't want you to be. Damn it, Barbara, I was only . . ."

She laughed and looked away. "You don't want any involvement, and apparently I can't get along without one. A rationalization? Is that what I have to have? It's a lousy price to pay. A whore's bargain, but maybe not quite as honest. But don't be completely pessimistic, dear Paul. Maybe when this is over, I can sell myself the idea it would be a nice dramatic gesture, a touching farewell."

"Why do you do this to yourself?"

She smiled directly into his eyes. "Because I'm a plain tiresome slob. Now sit still and let me work some of this off." She snapped her cap on and went to the pool so quickly it

was like escape. She dived cleanly. On these laps she drove
herself, her body riding higher in the water, making her kick
turns with a racing haste. He saw lightning in the east, fork-
ing down through the black sky under the thunderheads.

When she came back she was panting and gasping. She
half fell into the chair and leaned her head back and closed
her eyes. Her torso in the yellow sheath suit swelled and collapsed in the fast rhythm of her breathing.

"Now . . ." she said. "Tell me . . . if you found out . . .
anything new."

"I think I know who killed her."

She tensed and her eyes opened wide, and the hard surge
of her breathing changed, faltered, continued again. But
by the time he had finished all there was to tell, all the
guesses and the conjectures and hunches, there had been
more than enough time, many times over, for her to recover
from the strenuous exertion. She was hunched over, her elbows on her knees, head tilted sideways, looking at him with
a dazed, sick expression.

"And that man, too?"

"I don't know. I think so."

"But not for the money."

"I think she took the money. But I don't think it was the
main thing. She thinks . . . it was a good thing to do, to
kill them. And she probably had to kill Gable because he
suspected her. She's been very bold and very clever."

"But what will you do now, Paul?"

"The autopsy is going to bother Sheriff Walmo. I don't
have a single specific thing to go on. Doctor Nile accepts it
as a possibility, perhaps even a probability, but I don't think
anyone else in this area who knows her will be able to be
suspicious of her. She's such a . . . big, sunny, healthy kid.
Sam Kimber can't make himself believe it. I don't know
what I can do next. Look for the money. Try to trap her. I
don't know exactly. She's dangerous. I know that when I
look at her the next time I'm going to begin to doubt the whole
thing. And that is what makes her especially dangerous."

"You can tell from Lu's letter she thought there was something very odd about Angie Powell. She felt uneasy."

"So do I."

Barbara frowned and said, "Mr. Kimber would like to be
certain, one way or another, wouldn't he?"

"What do you mean?"

"He could lie to her, just to make sure, couldn't he? If she killed my sister because she was having an affair with Mr. Kimber, what would she do if Mr. Kimber told her I was going to stay down here and live with him?"

"I can't let you take a risk like that, Barbara."

"Why would it be such a risk? Lu and that Mr. Gable couldn't have known she was going to kill them. I know she might try to kill me."

"I don't like it."

"But you'll be here in case she tries, and you can stop her. Besides, what if you can't ever prove anything against her? What other way is there?"

"I'd rather set myself up as the next victim."

"How? Both Lucille and Mr. Gable were close to Sam Kimber. You're not. Why should she care what you do?"

"I still don't like it."

"You promised you'd let me help, Paul."

"This isn't what I had in mind."

"Can't we at least talk to Mr. Kimber about it?"

"I have to think about it, Barbara."

Suddenly they heard a faraway roaring sound. Looking to the east they saw the heavy curtain of rain coming toward them. They ran for cover into the thatched, three-walled structure beyond the end of the pool. The first fat drops began to fall before they reached it. The winds came, whipping the fringes of rain in toward them, sending them back into the far corner by some stacked tables and a pile of poolside mats. Within minutes it was dark and cool and they were isolated from the world by the hard hiss of the rain against the thatch overhead.

"If Mr. Kimber says yes, let me try," she shouted.

"If he says yes, and if you promise to do exactly as I say."

"I promise."

"I don't want you to be hurt."

"I'll be very careful, Paul. Really and truly careful."

# Eleven

STANIAL AND BARBARA Larrimore had arrived at the office building at seven-thirty in the morning and found the private entrance unlocked as Kimber had promised it would be.

Stanial parked his car a block away in case Angela Powell might notice it. Kimber had said she was in by eight many mornings.

Sam Kimber greeted them, wearing a flannel robe and slippers. "Morning," he said. "Can't get over feeling like a damn fool. What do you expect her to do? Pull a knife?"

"I expect her to follow the same pattern she did before. I think she made a date with Gus. I think she had an appointment with Lucille," Paul said. "She may be more reckless or more careful, but I think the pattern will be the same. And Barbara will be waiting wherever she says, and I'll be close enough to protect her."

Sam looked gaunt and red-eyed and listless. "You sound so damn sure of everything. You built this whole thing out of nothing."

"Not exactly nothing."

"As close as anybody can get to plain nothing and you know it. But I'm about as anxious to get her off your list as you are to prove she'd kill anybody. So we'll do it. But I swear I'm going to feel plain ridiculous."

"Do you think I'm enjoying it?" Barbara asked tartly.

Sam smiled at her. "Lu spoke right up to me too, honey."

"Where should I go to . . . get ready?" she asked.

"Through that door. It's the guest bedroom, Miss Barbara."

After Barbara was gone, Sam said, "Where's the best place to put on our little act?"

"The living room? Is there a place where I can watch?"

"Closet should be handy. And I better get out some ice and a bottle. Drinking is wicked, too."

Barbara came out of the guest bedroom. She had rumpled her hair and put on a bright crooked smear of lipstick. She wore her robe over a frilly nightgown. She was barefoot. She looked sullen and bawdy. "Will I do?"

Sam Kimber shook his head and marveled at her. "Girl, you look like we've been living here a week without sticking a head outdoors."

Barbara curled up in a corner of the leather couch in the living room. Sam Kimber paced the floor. Paul found the precise angle of the closet door where he could see the most without being seen.

At twenty after eight Sam listened at the door and then turned to them. He took a swallow of his drink. "That's her. Nobody else can run a typewriter that fast. Pick your drink up, Miss Barbara. I'll play this by ear."

As soon as Paul was in position, Sam opened the door between the apartment and the ante-office and said heartily, "Morning, Angie. Come on in here a minute." Paul saw the big girl come smiling through the door, and saw the smile disappear instantly.

"Angie, this here is Barbara Larrimore and she's Lucille's kid sister and I wanted you two gals should know each other."

"How do you do," Barbara said in a slurred and husky voice. Angela Powell nodded. She stood straight, obedient, waiting.

"Barbie is going to be around a lot from now on, and she's going to be here a long time, and you're going to run into her frequent, Angie. So what I wanted to say to you, anything Miss Larrimore needs or wants, and I'm not around, she just mentions it to you, and it's like the orders came straight from me."

"My glass is empty again, lover," Barbara said.

"You got the message, Angie?" Sam said.

"Yes, Mister Sam," she said in a low voice.

"You want she should do anything for you right now, honey?" Sam asked.

"When I think of something, lover, I'll let her know. See you around, Angie."

"Is that all, Mister Sam?"

"All for now. Maybe I'll be in the office later on. Maybe not."

Angie made a military about face and walked out, her head high. The door hissed slowly shut and the lock hatch clicked.

Stanial came out of the closet. The three of them glanced at each other with an obvious uneasiness.

"Paul, she didn't look at me once. She looked past me but not at me. Paul, are you . . . really sure? She looks so . . . sweet and decent."

"It sure turned all her lights right off," Sam said sadly. "It hurt her real bad. You could see that. Like sticking a knife in her. You know, after you find out for yourself this whole thing is wrong, Paul, I'm going to tell Angie just how and why we did her this way. She'll understand. She's a quick bright girl."

Barbara quietly left the room. As soon as she was gone, Stanial said, "Be a little careful yourself, Sam."

"You serious?"

"You're a sinner. Maybe you just lost your immunity."

Sam sat down. "I have the feeling I've lost just about everything else in this world. Now what do we do? Just wait?"

"If she's as unbalanced as I think she is, we won't have long to wait."

"She knows where Barbara is staying. I mentioned it the other day."

"I'll stay close to her."

"She looks like a good girl. She looks soft at you, Paul."

"I like her."

"If she's anything like Lu, you got you a hundred and ten per cent woman."

"All I've got is a client, Sam."

Barbara came out in her street clothes, carrying the overnight case. She made a face and said, "I feel as if I'd been on call." She shook her head. "That girl has such a nice expression."

"But it's like a strong magnet. Every compass needle in the area points right at her. It has to be more than coincidence."

"Knew an old boy in Miami one time looked like a bishop," Sam said. "Cleanest white hair you ever saw. A right saintly expression. Didn't drink, smoke or cuss. Always dressed nice. Real quiet. Made a nice living swindling retired folks, selling them imaginary cemetery plots in a ten-acre swamp he owned."

After some aimless, uneasy talk, Paul took Barbara back to the motel. He had moved to room six, adjacent to but not adjoining hers. He went to her room with her. They sat in silence for a little while, and she said, "With an absolutely spotless conscience, that girl still made me feel sleazy."

"You looked sleazy."

"Maybe that's my undiscovered talent, up till now."

"I'm wondering just when and how you'll hear from her."

"I don't think I will. If she is what you think she is, then she'd be too smart to fall for this. You let her know you suspected her. She won't risk anything for a long time."

"Unless she's very sure of herself. Why shouldn't she be? Everything has worked so far. They get a feeling of invincibility."

"They?"

"The unbalanced ones. They hear voices. They follow orders. She'll hear instructions about you. By now, or pretty soon, Sam will go into the office and say you've gone back to the motel. She'll think about it. She'll think of something.

And then you'll hear from her. And it will be something plausible."

"You seem so very sure, Paul."

"She didn't waste any time over Gus Gable."

"So we just wait?"

"With the patience of a cop or a thief."

"How long?"

"Until midnight tomorrow if we have to."

"And then what?"

"Then I think of some way to nudge her, to force her to make a move."

# Twelve

AT TEN-THIRTY Angie Powell walked slowly into Sam's office, closed the door behind her, approached the desk, sat in the chair beside the desk and stared at Sam with a deadness and a despair.

"Something wrong?" he asked.

"About ever'thing is going wrong, Mister Sam."

"How do you mean?"

She closed her eyes for a few moments, gave a heavy sigh and brushed the dark gold hair back from her temple with the back of her hand. "I just can't work for you any more."

"Why not?"

"You got another woman now, younger than the other one, before the other one is complete cold in her grave. And this time there's just no excuse at all."

"What business is it of yours?"

She looked at him sadly. "It's like it gives me more than I can do, Mister Sam. It keeps piling up. A person thinks they've got everything straightened out, and then there's more. You've been good to me. But I've got to just get away from you before I have to punish you too."

It took several seconds for the full significance of what she had said to make its mark upon him. He felt a coldness along his spine. He looked at her and saw no awareness of guilt. Just a weary resignation.

"Angie, girl, did you . . . punish Lucille?"

"Lucille and Gus. Both of them."

"But *why*?" he whispered.

She looked mildly startled. "They were black with sin, weren't they? She led you into evil ways. And Gus was a liar and a whoremonger. I used to think of you as just being weak, Mister Sam. Not wicked. Stealing from the government and being ready to run with the stolen money so as you wouldn't have to give up that woman. And I was told I could save you by taking temptation out of your path, taking away the woman and the money."

"You were told."

"They were marked out to me," she said with a strange pride.

"Angie, Angie. My God, you don't understand what you've done."

"This morning I looked on you and saw the face of evil again, and because you've been good to me, I've got to get away from you before you're marked out in turn for punishment."

"But you're going to have to be . . . put where you can't hurt people."

She sighed again. "If that's what they want to do to me."

"Do you want to come with me now and talk to Harv Walmo about Lucille and Gus?"

"I don't mind. I can't seem to care much about anything this morning, Mister Sam. But I guess you should get that money back."

"Where is it?"

"In that pond out to your shack. I put it in a canister and sunk it out there, and I can show you where. That Stanial man, he guessed I've been punishing people. I could tell by looking at him. If he could meet us out there, I could get that money for you and I could tell the both of you the whole thing, how it happened. I don't much take to talking to Harv Walmo. Mister Sam, if I told you and Mr. Stanial, then could you tell it all to Harv?"

"Yes. Angie, do you know what you've done? Did you know I was going to marry Lucille?"

"Would that make sin smell any the sweeter? Why don't you call that Mr. Stanial right now and have him meet us out there. I could hide it from everybody else, but I couldn't hide it from him."

"Could I have Harv meet us out there, too?"

"Enough later so I can have time to tell you all about it."

He noticed his hand was wet when he picked up the

phone. They rang Stanial's room. He answered on the sixth ring.

"This is Sam."

"I heard it ringing from next door, Sam."

"It . . . it's all over."

"You sound strange."

"I feel strange. She wants to tell us all about it. Out at my shack. She dropped the money in my pond out there. It's about a forty-minute trip. You go out state road nine-twenty and it's the third dirt road to the right past Garner Corners. It's a private road, all marked. We'll meet you out there."

"In an hour, tell him," Angie said.

"In an hour. Can you make it all right?"

"I'll leave Barbara here."

"The Sheriff is going to meet us out there too, Paul."

"Did she . . . just come in and tell you?"

"Just like that. See you out there."

Sam hung up. He looked at Angie. She sat placidly, her hands in her lap. "They didn't do anything to you, Angie, either one of them."

"It wasn't a personal matter," she explained. She yawned. "Since starting to tell about it, it seems I can't stop yawning. Mister Sam, before you call Harv, you want to see where I put the rest of the money, the part I couldn't pack into that canister?"

"Where is it?"

She gestured back over her shoulder. "I hid it in your place. I guess you'd never find it, I didn't show you."

He stood up, thinking that he could not truly believe it until he held some of the money in his hands. Then maybe he could comprehend the bland horror of it.

She stood up too and said, "Please don't act different going by Mrs. Nimmits. She'll know all about it soon enough. I guess we could go on down in your elevator. You could call Harv on the apartment phone."

He nodded. The thing to do was get it over with. She stopped at her desk and picked up her straw purse. He held the door for her, and as they went into the apartment he noticed, with a curious feeling of horror, that she had resumed her normal glowing smile for the benefit of Mrs. Nimmits.

The door swung shut. "Well, where is it? You can stop smiling now."

"In the bathroom. Please don't speak ugly to me, Mister Sam."

They went to the bathroom. He flicked on the white dazzle of fluorescence. "There's no place to hide money in here," he said.

"Yes, there is. I packed it right in back of that panel up there." She pointed to the wall above the wide tiled counter. He stood beside her.

"Panel?" he said.

She took a quick step back and, holding the straw envelope purse by one end, she slammed it against the side of his head. In the weighted end of the straw purse was one of the flat lead weights she had removed from one of the canvas pockets of her quick-release belt she used for skin-diving. She had gone down to her car at nine o'clock, opened the trunk, removed the weight and placed it in her purse. Sam Kimber took two tottering steps and went down onto his hands and knees. She struck him again, with less haste and more precision, and he folded down against the floor. She put the purse on the counter, stepped around him and turned on both faucets in the oversized, sunken tub. As the water roared into the tub she squatted beside Sam and worked her hand into the right pocket and took his keys out. She put the keys in her purse. She straightened up. Her mouth felt stiff with disapproval. Mister Sam had been very proud of this bathroom. She had heard him snickering and smirking about the seven-foot tub and the shower stall big enough for three or four people. She knew it must have been the scene of orgies beyond her comprehension. Mister Sam, with his cheek resting on a colorful mat, looked as if he were sleeping. He looked younger. There was almost a look of innocence about him. She felt a sad regret, knowing it was too late for him, too late for any weakening of her resolution. Now the list was long and there was much to do.

Soon the tub was more than half full. She turned the water off and stood in the steamy silence and felt the first slow inner pulsing of delight, those red mare flexures which blurred the severity of the Joan-feeling. She straddled him, grasped him by the armpits and slid him, head first, over the low squared-off rim of the big tub. She knelt on the mat and thrust him the rest of the way, turning him the long way of the tub, face down. She put her right hand firmly yet almost caressingly on the corded nape of his neck and pushed his head deep. She felt the bubbles tickle past her fingers. She thought this would be less than the others, but quite suddenly he began such a thrashing series of violent spasms, it took all her strength to hold him. And her hot blindness came then, taking her far away. She came back slowly, aware of the deepening of her breath, of the fading heat of her body, and realized Mister Sam had been motionless for quite a long time. She released him and stood up. Her legs were very weak and she felt slightly dizzy. She dried her hand and forearm on a thick towel. She looked down at him. He was slightly wavery because the water was still moving a little bit. As she watched it grew still.

She picked up her purse and turned the lights off as she left the bathroom. She sat quietly in the living room with her eyes closed until she felt strong again, and then she stood up and began smiling and pushed the big door open and walked out into the ante-office. Holding the door she turned and said, "I'll sure tell her, Mister Sam." She went to Mrs. Nimmits' desk and said, "Mister Sam isn't feeling so good and he's going to see if he can get some sleep, and he doesn't want anybody disturbing him for anything. He's sent me out to the shack to get some papers he left out there, so you hold the fort, huh?"

"Sure, Angie."

"In case you should wonder, I'm taking his car."

"Okay, Angie."

She went down in the public elevator and walked around to the parking lot in the rear. She took Sam's keys from her purse and moved his big beige Imperial over close to her car. She opened her trunk and took her canvas bag of gear and moved it into the Chrysler. It contained swim suit, swim fins, two masks, harness, diving belt and spare regulator.

On the way out of town she stopped at Scotty's Marine to pick up her twin tanks.

"Got you a day off and the boss' car too, huh?" Scotty said.

"Maybe not the whole day off. How about that regulator?"

"I cleaned it and adjusted it and it checks out fine. No charge, Angie. And I put filling the two tanks on your bill. Let me help you with those. I swear, Angie, you carry those the way most women would carry a pocketbook. Who you diving with?"

"Alone again, Scotty."

"Now you know better than that! It's dangerous."

"But I'm very careful, Scotty, honest."

"Look. It's a slow day. I'll close up and come along. Take me one minute to get ready."

"No thanks," she said, and pulled out, the tires skidding on the gravel, waving back at him after she had straightened out on the highway.

She drove the big car as fast as she dared. At the shack she got out and swung the gate open and left it open. She drove through a half mile of white pine and when she reached the house, she swung around it and drove on and parked beside Sam's ten-acre pond. The water was so high in the pond there was less than a foot of clearance under the narrow weathered dock. She laid her gear out in an orderly manner, stripped down and pulled her faded blue swim suit on. The black mosquitoes whined around her. She stowed her clothing in the gear bag along with the excess equipment and flipped it into the car. She hooked the tanks to the harness and shouldered it on and buckled it. She buckled the weighted belt around her waist, over the harness straps, snapped the fin straps snugly against her ankles, picked up her mask and went flapping out to the end of the narrow dock and lowered herself heavily. The tanks thumped against the dock. She spat into her mask, dipped it into the water and swirled it clean. She put the mask on, adjusted the regulator, bit down on the mouthpiece and turned and fell backwards into the pond. She twisted underwater and straightened out and explored. The water was not as murky as she had expected it would be. In the middle where it seemed to average twelve feet of depth, she could still see reasonably well in the saffron world. At the end of the dock it was six feet deep.

When exploration was done, she went under the dock. It was shadowy under there, and she found a level where she could stand with the fins against the soft muck of the bottom and the water barely covering her shoulders. She pushed the mask up onto her forehead and took the mouthpiece out. She held onto a cross brace to support herself.

As she waited with a mild almost bovine patience, she sorted out the possibilities of what could be done about Lucille's sister, once Stanial was out of the way. In the dead of night she could get Mister Sam down and out the private door and into his car, with that suitcase he kept packed. And the sister would come if she thought Sam wanted her. She could go into the trunk with Sam, alive or dead, it made little difference, and there were three real deep places at Lake Larra where you could get a car close enough. Mister Sam wanted to go on a trip with a woman.

Five minutes after Paul Stanial had driven away from the motel, Barbara decided to ignore his instructions. It seemed so ineffectual to sit in a motel room while the whole thing was being solved and settled. Sit and wait and wonder, with the night lock on and stern orders not to open the door to anyone.

She phoned Sheriff Walmo. "This is Barbara Larrimore," she said. "I'm so glad I caught you before you left, Sheriff."

"I beg your pardon?"

"I employed a man named Mr. Paul Stanial to . . ."

"Yes, I know all about that, Miss Larrimore. And I guess if that's the way you want to spend your money . . ."

"Sheriff, I wonder if I could ride out there with you."

"Ride out where, Miss?"

"Why, out to that place in the woods Mr. Kimber owns."

"Out to Sam's shack? Now why would I be going out there?"

"Didn't Mr. Kimber even get in touch with you yet? He called Mr. Stanial over a half hour ago. And then he was going to call you to meet him out there. Angela Powell apparently confessed to murdering my sister. And Mr. Gable. And she hid something in a pond out there, and she is going out with Mr. Kimber to show him where it is, and Mr. Stanial was going to meet them out there. Sheriff? Sheriff Walmo!"

"I'm here, Miss. I'm here and I'm wondering if you're drunk."

"I am *not* drunk. And now I'm worried about why Mr. Kimber didn't call you. Mr. Stanial believes Miss Powell is . . . some kind of a fanatic and very very dangerous."

"Angie Powell?"

"I *wish* you would stop making those gasping sounds and do something. I know Mr. Stanial has gone out there."

"And Sam Kimber told Stanial all this . . . this information?"

"He certainly did!"

"What's your number there? I'll talk to Sam and call you back."

She paced the floor. It was a long wait before the phone

rang. "Miss Larrimore? There should be a deputy pulling in there any minute to pick you up. Then he'll pick me up here and we'll go on out and see what's going on."

"Didn't Mr. Kimber confirm what I told you?"

"Tell you in the car," Walmo said and hung up. She went outside and saw a county car parked by the office with a man in uniform just getting out of it. She hurried to him and identified herself and got in.

When they stopped at the court house, Sheriff Walmo came out and got into the front seat beside her.

"Right on out nine-twenty, Pete," he said, slamming the car door. "This is kind of a wild story, Miss Larrimore."

"Didn't you get hold of Mr. Kimber?"

"I got hold of Miz Nimmits in Sam's office. She said Sam don't feel so good and he's taking a nap. And she said Angie went off a while back in Sam's car. Miss Larrimore, sometimes a man like this Stanial, they get just a little bit carried away trying to make it look like there's leads worth working on."

"Paul isn't like that!"

"Until they get themselves worked into a corner and have to take off."

"Doctor Nile told Paul Stanial it was quite possible that girl is dangerous."

"Stanial told you that Doc Nile said that. It doesn't have to mean Nile said it, Miss."

She turned to look angrily at him. "And did Mr. Stanial just *imagine* that the autopsy on Mr. Gable is very odd?"

Walmo's large face darkened. "Somebody is doing too much talking, by God."

"Is anybody making any attempt to disturb Sam Kimber and ask him to verify what I told you?"

Walmo lifted the dashboard mike off its hook. "Car three, car three, calling in. You picking me up okay, Henry? Over."

"Loud and clear, Shurf."

"Henry, you figure Billy has had time to get to Sam Kimber's office yet? Over."

"He should be there right about now, Shurf."

"Then you phone there and get Billy and tell him I want Sam shook awake no matter how much hell he has to raise, and put Sam through on a phone link to me right in this here car fast as he can. Over."

"I'll have Billy do just that, Shurf."

"Over and out," Walmo said and hung up.

"Shouldn't we . . . be going faster?" Barbara asked tentatively.

"We go faster, Miss, and we're too soon out of the reach of this danged old-timey radio. Three years I been after better, but the County Commissioners they chop my budget down every year."

They rode sedately into the country on the black, narrow, lumpy surface of state road nine-twenty.

"Calling car three, calling car three," a tinny little insect voice said. "You still hear me, Shurf?"

"I hear you, Henry. Over."

"Shurf, Billy he busted in, but nobody's going to shake Mister Sam awake. Son of a bitch. Mister Sam, he's face down drowned in his own bathtub with his clothes on. Son of a bitch. You better come right on back, Shurf."

Sheriff Walmo hung the mike up without a word. "Unwind this here thing, Pete," he ordered. And the sudden acceleration tilted Barbara's head back.


Paul Stanial saw Sam Kimber's car beyond the house beside a sizeable pond, and he drove down in its tracks and parked behind it. He got out into the back country silence. He could hear a liquid sound of meadow larks, and a distant swamp-sound of frogs. He slapped a mosquito and rubbed it off the side of his throat.

"Sam!" he called. "Hey, Sam!"

There was no response. He walked back to the house. It seemed to be closed up. He pounded the back door with his fist and listened again to silence. He walked back down to the pond and leaned into his car and gave a long blast on the horn. He stood and looked at the pond, wondering what to do next. A skiff half full of water was tied to the narrow dock. Weeds grew tall around the shore, but the water looked clean.

There seemed to him to be an ominous quality in the silence. It gave him the feeling that something had happened to Sam Kimber, that he might even be nestled in the mud and grass at the bottom of the pond.

He walked out onto the narrow dock. He stood at the end of it and looked at the surface of the pond. A small fish made a feeding circle.

As he turned around, there was a great startling swashing

sound close beside the dock, and before he could turn to see what it was, his ankles were grabbed and yanked from under him. He fell heavily, striking his shoulder and the side of his head against the dock boards. He made a dazed grab and missed the dock. The smash of cool water cleared his head and he tried to kick his legs free and swim to the dock. But even as he stroked he could see he was being pulled out toward the center of the pond. He twisted and saw half the face mask above the water, saw the soaked cap of dark gold, the lavender eyes behind glass, narrowed and intent. He used the leverage of her grasp on his ankles to double himself and try to reach her with his hands, but she released him. The moment he tried to swim away from her, the powerful hands closed once more on his ankles and began drawing him back.

Three times he reached for her, three times she released him, and each time the dock was farther away. But the next time she grabbed his ankles, she pulled him down, pulled him under. He doubled down to try to grab her wrists, but she let go of him. He bobbed up, caught his breath and was immediately yanked under again. And suddenly he knew how Lucille Hanson had been drowned without a mark on her. There could be but one ending to this one-sided struggle. Exhaustion, panic and death.

And so, the next time she released him, he bobbed up, filled his lungs, doubled, spun and drove down at her as powerfully as he could. He reached and grasped something, some edge of fabric, but as he reached for her with his other hand, she tore loose. With his eyes open in the yellow murk he strained to reach her, only to see her, sleek and golden brown, turn beyond his grasp to cruise in a half circle, graceful, watchful and immune as a shark, the flippers thrusting her faster than he could have swum even unencumbered by clothing. And as he fought up toward the light and the air, he knew, with a sick despair, that there was no more chance to reason with her than there would have been with a shark.

She drew him down before he could reach the surface, and with a great effort he wrenched one foot free and kicked blindly down at her, but missed her, felt fingertips brush his ankle and fasten there again. His lungs were beginning to spasm in the involuntary attempt to draw the air in, and he kept his throat locked only through a final effort of will. He knew he was being pulled deeper, and he doubled once more, feeling for her wrists. Before he could touch them he was freed, and grasped once again as he tried to straighten. It was too far and too long, and his throat opened, the air expelled in a noisy metallic eruption and the lungs sucked full of the yellow water. At once he was in a languid and drifting dream wherein, if he cared to make the effort to climb it with his watery limbs, there was a ladder going straight up, its rungs made of wide yellow bands of satin, cleverly graded to increasingly pale hues as it reached up toward the surface.

As he felt himself fading, like a light going off, he had a faraway awareness that she had climbed his body, was now close to him, holding him. He felt hard fingers digging into his back. She had twined sleek strong legs about his dying, drifting ones. And, seeing her vaguely in the yellow light, he felt a mild fascination in seeing that she was leaning back, her face strangely savage, holding him, churning her hips against him in a monstrous and murderous parody of the sexual act. And he knew she would leave him here in the yellow world and go after Barbara next. His hands were free. He brought his right hand up in front of his face. He turned the edge of it toward her throat so it would slice readily through the water. He chopped that straining throat as hard as he could. She drifted away in his dream, sinking, turning, erupting a bloat of bubbles. She brushed his leg. He put a languid foot against her and pushed. Suddenly he broke into a blackening world and spewed a great gout of water, choking, gasping, flailing with an increasing pain and panic that made him wish he had not been thrust up out of the yellow dream below him. He coughed and gagged and choked, but the sky brightened and he saw the dock at the far end of the world and began to paddle his way toward it, coughing, vomiting, half-blinded, moving with an earnest, dogged instinct.

She came thrashing to the surface a scant yard in front of him, foaming and spinning like some great wounded fish. She steadied and turned toward him. She had lost her mask. It was an animal face, emptied of reason and mercy, but he saw the hand tuck the mouthpiece in place. She lunged and caught his wrist and took him down. He struck at her with his fist, caught a strap, pulled her close, saw her in the brighter yellow near the surface, her strong breasts bared where the suit had been torn away, saw the breathing tube and yanked it out of her mouth. They burst up into the air again, entwined and thrashing, and then she took him down into darkness ...

He coughed and gagged and gushed water against the rough boards and tried to tell them to stop. But the iron pressure kept coming down on the small of his back and then going away. He coughed again and reached and caught an edge of gray board and tried to pull himself away from the thing that was injuring him. And it stopped then. He groaned and rolled onto his side. He opened his eyes and looked into a blurred distortion of Barbara's face. It was vivid with concern and alarm. She touched his cheek. She said something with darling in it. He tried to sit up and they tried to stop him, but he pushed them away. He looked at Barbara. "How'd you get soaking wet this time?" he asked in a husky rasp.

Sheriff Walmo was suddenly beside her, shaking his head in mournful wonder. "Saw the two of you thrashing out there as we stopped. Barely got the car door open and this gal come busting by me like a rocket. Just as you go under, she goes off the end of that dock. Never see any human person go so fast in the water in my life. I swear to God, she made a wake you could hear crash up against the shore."

"Are you all right? Are you all right, Paul?" Barbara asked earnestly.

He tried to shake like a wet dog. It was partially a shudder. "She tried to drown me."

"Making a habit of it," Walmo said. "Drowned Sam, too."

"Here?" Paul asked blankly.

"No. Right in that big special bathtub he was so proud of."

"Where is she?"

"Right over there," Walmo said.

Paul tried to stand. Walmo and Barbara helped him up. As he straightened another spasm of coughing shook him. They supported him. The tears ran down his face. When he'd blinked his vision clear he saw Angie Powell huddled on the ground, her wrists handcuffed around a sapling. Her equipment was scattered nearby. She wore one fin, the bottom portion of her torn blue suit and her tank harness. Her wet hair was pasted to her skull and across half her face. One eye was visible. It looked through them and beyond them, like the indifferent eye of a caged animal.

Paul saw movement out of the corner of his eye and turned

to see a deputy approaching with a blanket in his hand.

Walmo said, "Now, Pete, I'm getting right tired of you just standing and staring at her."

Pete spat and said, "Well, you got to admit she . . ."

"Shut up. I tell you, Stanial, it was a day's work getting her this far."

"How did you get her in?"

"Poled this here old skiff out to where the excitement was. Had to chunk her on the head twice with the pole before we could haul her into the skiff. By then Miss Larrimore had you towed to shore. Pete went to respirate you and I was getting this stuff off Angie when she came to and bit me twice and started to take off, and Pete came running and tackled her. And she bit him once and liked to kick his face off before we cuffed her up there."

Pete bent cautiously and tried to tuck the blanket around her, but she snapped at him like an animal. There was an audible click of teeth when she missed him. Pete jumped back.

"We got to get back in, Pete," Walmo said. "You got that persuader out of the car, so you just chunk her on the head again."

Pete waved the braided leather sap and looked at the girl helplessly. Walmo grunted and went over. Barbara turned her back. Walmo took the sap and bent and struck Angie quite delicately behind the ear. Her eye rolled up and she sagged against the ground. The two men removed the cuffs, wrapped her in the blanket, carried her and put her in the cage rear of the county car and recuffed her to the big ring bolt.

In a few minutes the three-car caravan headed back toward the city. Walmo drove Sam Kimber's car. Pete drove the county car. Barbara drove Paul's car.

Stanial sat beside her with his eyes shut. "I thought I'd had it."

"So did I . . . think you'd had it," Barbara said in a very small voice.

"She was hiding under the dock. She yanked me off."

"How horrible!"

"You came right out after us?"

"I didn't even have time to think. I dived and found you and took you away from her."

"How?"

"I just don't know. She kept trying to grab us. I kept fighing her off. Then the boat came. She wasn't like anything human."

"But she is. They shouldn't have kept hitting her on the head."

"We couldn't stop them."

"We didn't try."

"I didn't particularly want to try," Barbara said with precise savagery.


Doctor Rufus Nile was waiting for them at the hospital. As soon as he had drugged Angela Powell and ordered her put in restraint, he checked Stanial over, gave him a prescription to be filled and ordered him to bed at the motel.

"I'll come by this evening and look you over. We'll just watch out for pneumonia or some kind of lung infection, Stanial. You keep an eye on him, Miss Larrimore. What you have to watch for is . . ."

"Doc! Doc Nile!" a great screeching voice called, filling the corridor outside the emergency room. The huge woman filled the doorway. "What kind of nonsense am I hearing? They're telling lies about Angie. Where is my little girl? What have you done to my little girl?"

Doctor Nile, moving with a slow dignity unlike his normal movements, moved toward her. "Done to her? None of us have done anything to her, Mary. The thing that was done to her—*you* did, a long long time ago."


Doctor Nile stopped at the motel at nine. He looked and acted weary.

He sat beside the bed and said, "What a mess! What a stinking mess! This town will talk about nothing else for weeks. Months. Anyhow, I got her to talking calmly enough. Not rationally. Just calmly. They took it all down. The state's attorney can look the transcript over and bring in somebody else to see if she can stand trial. I'd say no. I hope they don't try to go through with it."

"What will happen to her?" Barbara asked.

"Criminally insane is a pretty broad term. It covers a heap of things. They'll probably say she's some kind of a classic case, once they figure out the right name to call it. But clever enough. It was going to be fixed to look like Sam run off with you, Miss Larrimore. And nobody was ever going to find

Stanial or his car. Not five murders. Five punishments. For sin."

"But you would have guessed," Paul said to Nile.

"And guessed right and maybe got myself killed too. Kill the sinners and it looks like you have to clean out the whole world. Hah? But she got rid of three before her luck ran out. And Walmo says it would have been four if you hadn't gotten him stirred up."

"Or five," Barbara said. She frowned. "I should hate her, but I can't. It's as if Lucille was struck by lightning."

"She just got there first. They had a date to talk about something. She parked in the next road down, went out in her skin-diving outfit and was out there in the deep water waiting when your sister swam out. She just pulled her down. Then she swam back to where she'd parked, took the gear off, went through the woods, took the apartment key and then she drove on back to town and went back to work. She did it on her lunch hour. She went and got the money that night. Went out a window after her folks were asleep."

"Where is the money?"

"She took it into the woods and burned it all. It was sinful money, she says. Poor Gus Gable got squeezed unconscious and then she stuck her hand up under his ribs and gave his heart a squeeze and turned him loose in his car. And went back through that same window into her room. She clunked Sam on the head with her pocketbook with a piece of lead in it, and slid him into his sunken tub. But she was following what she was put here to do, she says." Nile sighed again. "I can turn over a pretty good case history, I guess. She was fighting something inside herself and she took it out on the world."

"How is she now?"

"Quiet. Relaxed. Doesn't know what's coming next and doesn't much care. That girl has a nice pleasant disposition."

"Everybody likes her," Stanial said. "Everybody likes Angie."

"News people here from Miami and Jacksonville already," Nile said.

"I had to tell the desk we're not taking any calls," Barbara said. "I don't know what to say to them. What can I tell them? I called my aunt and my mother and I told them. They wanted to know why. There isn't any why. The plane went down. The car skidded. Life is going to be a tricky thing, isn't it, no matter what or where? How can you sidestep everything?" Her voice had gotten thin.

"Give you a little pill, too?" Nile said.

She shivered slightly and straightened her shoulders. "No. I'm all right. Thank you."

Nile jumped to his feet. "Well. You have the number. Any fever starts, any difficulty breathing, you phone. Hah? Good."

In a midnight dream Stanial was back in the yellow deep, and around him swam the orange-brown girl, around and around, naked, without equipment, hair streaming wild, face severe and remote, moving sleekly with each pump of a powerful thigh, the long muscles of her back reaching, the bubbles streaming up and back from parted thoughtful lips as she breathed.

The dream jolted him awake and he heard the echo of a sound he had made in sleep. Barbara had put a thick towel over the shade of a small lamp in the far corner of the room, and she got up from a chair and came toward him to lay the inside of her wrist across his forehead.

"Are you all right?" she asked in a low voice.

"Just a dream."

"Are you breathing all right?"

He took two deep breaths. "Yes. You don't have to stay here."

"I'd rather. I don't mind. Go to sleep, Paul."

She went back to the chair.

"I keep thinking of a funny thing. An odd thing," he said.

"Yes."

"When I was convinced I was finished, I had this . . . terrible feeling of irritation. Like wanted to say to her, 'Not now! Not while I'm like this.'"

"Like what, dear?"

"Like being an impostor, I guess. Not doing what I should be doing. Maybe most of the people in the world feel that way. I thought I could get along in this kind of work. I can. But it's sort of like a career navy guy taking a job as a hired skipper of a private boat. Next week I'll probably be checking out some plaintiff in an auto case to find out if the neck brace is window trimming or if he really wears it all the time. I don't know. It just seemed to be a hell of a thing—to die when you're not in your own line of work."

"So you'll change it."

"I . . . I guess so. Back where I belong."

"Thanks to Angie?"

"You could put it that way."

"Try to sleep, Paul."

When he awoke again the room was full of a gray light. She was standing by the window, with the look of someone who had been standing, looking out for a long time. No dream had awakened him this time.

"Barbara?"

She started, came quickly to him. When she felt his forehead he took her hand, tugged gently so that she sat on the edge of the bed.

"There's something else," he said. "When I was going, sort of fading away, there was the thought of you. And enough life in that thought to bring me back a little, make a final effort."

"Yes?"

"So the involvement began then. Whether I wanted it or not. But maybe you're still free. I wouldn't know."

Her hand rested in his for a long time. And then she sighed and leaned down to him and put her mouth on his. In the gentleness of that kiss he ran his hand along a firm plane of her back, and she shivered and let the round girl weight of her come slowly onto his chest, and dug then into a deeper sweetness of that kiss. She placed her cheek against his and held him and shivered again and said, "Now you know about me."

"Barbara. Darling. This isn't just a . . ."

She put her fingers across his lips. "I don't want to strike bargains. I don't want to dicker. Not yet, anyway." She kissed him again, and laughed aloud, a strange, small laugh of triumph. "Look what I towed ashore!" she said. "Are you well enough?"

"No fever."

"We'll change that," she whispered. And his girl stood up in the gray light and, turning half away from him, began to undress. She moved deliberately, with no flavor of coyness or enticement. In the silver light her expression was thoughtful, her lips curved into a shape that was on the edge of smiling, yet marked with a sadness. She turned, took one meek and hesitant step, then hastened the rest of the way into waiting arms—a creature complex and glorious and rewarding, demanding of him now and forever nothing less than a total commitment, willingly given.